D0407693

A SONG FOR MY MOTHER

A *Song* FOR MY *Mother*

KAT MARTIN

Vanguard Press
A Member of the Perseus Books Group

Published by Vanguard Press
A Member of the Perseus Books Group

Designed by Brent Wilcox
Set in 12 point Fairfield Light

Library of Congress Cataloging-in-Publication Data
Martin, Kat.
  A song for my mother / Kat Martin.
    p.   cm.
  ISBN 978-1-59315-656-5 (alk. paper)
  1. Mothers and daughters—Fiction.
2. Grandmothers—Fiction.   3. Michigan—Fiction.
4. Domestic fiction.   I. Title.
  PS3563.A7246S66 2011
  813'.54--dc22
                                        2010045247

Vanguard Press books are available at special discounts for
bulk purchases in the U.S. by corporations, institutions,
and other organizations. For more information, please
contact the Special Markets Department at the Perseus
Books Group, 2300 Chestnut Street, Suite 200,
Philadelphia, PA19103, or call (800) 810-4145, ext. 5000,
or e-mail special.markets@perseusbooks.com.

10 9 8 7 6 5 4 3 2 1

For my mother.

Mom, I miss you every day.

A SONG FOR MY MOTHER

*I wrote a song for my mother, but I never
played the notes. It spoke of the love I felt
for her, my gratitude for all she had done.
It told her how much I owed her for
the years of her life she gave me.*

*I wrote a song for my mother,
but I never sang the words.*

*Now she is gone and the song
is only a fading memory, a soft ache
that reminds me of the unsung melody
locked away in my heart.*

Dreyerville, Michigan
April 1995

Marilys Hanson didn't want to go home. It was Katie, her ten-year-old daughter, who wanted to visit Dreyerville, the small Michigan town where Marly had been raised. Katie had begged for months to finally meet the grandmother she had never known. Marly had finally agreed.

The day was cool but sunny, a light breeze blowing over the fields and whispering through the verdant forests at the edge of town. Main Street loomed ahead. Unable to resist a look at the place she had left behind twelve years ago, Marly pressed on the brake, slowing her old blue Ford sedan to make the turn. It was a beautiful little town, like something out of a picture book with its sycamore-lined streets, old domed courthouse, and ornate clock tower in the middle of the square.

She remembered Tremont's Antiques in the block to her left, and next to it, Brenner's Bakery. She and her mom had made it a tradition to go to the bakery on Saturday mornings. Marly could almost see Mrs. Culver standing behind the glass counter in her pink-and-white uniform, her gray-blond hair tucked neatly beneath a matching pink cap, smiling and chatting as she took their order. The place smelled of yeast and cinnamon, and patrons sat at little round, white wrought-iron tables.

Of course, that was all before.

Braking again, she turned the car onto Fir Street. This time of year, the entire town was a lush garden of shrubs and plants, the trees all leafed out, the grass so green it made your eyes hurt.

She drove a couple of blocks and pulled up to the curb in front of a gray-and-white, wood-frame house built in the twenties, the paint a little faded and in places starting to peel. Katie slept in the passenger seat, her head tilted against the window. Looking at her daughter, Marly felt a tug at her heart. Katie was the best thing that had ever happened to her. She was sweet and smart and loving.

And Marly had almost lost her.

Reaching down, she turned off the engine, sat for long moments just staring at the house that had once been her home. The house she had fled that awful night.

After so many years, just being in Dreyerville made her stomach churn. Where she gripped the steering wheel, her palms were sweating. Her pulse thumped dully. Years of emotional turmoil threatened to surface. Marly took mental hold of herself and firmly tamped it down.

She had made the decision to come. Now she was here. For Katie, she would handle it.

She took a deep breath and slowly released it. She hadn't seen her mother since the night she had left twelve years ago, the night she had run off with Burly Hanson, one of the town bad boys. Even when they were dating, Burly drank too much and flirted with other women, but she wasn't afraid of him and Marly was desperate to escape. When Burly offered to marry her and take her out of Dreyerville, she had jumped at the chance.

She had sworn that night she would never return, but she had a daughter to think of now, a child who had just survived a series of brutal radiation and chemotherapy treatments for brain cancer. Still fast asleep, Katie breathed softly, her bald head gleaming in the sunlight slanting down through the window.

Marly had considered shaving off her own shoulder-length blond hair the way people did when a loved one was fighting the disease, but Katie had begged her not to.

"Please don't do it, Mom. It'll only remind me how ugly I look."

So instead, Marly had tamed the soft curls that were her secret vanity into a modest French braid and silently thanked her brave little girl.

She glanced again at the child sleeping peacefully next to her. The prognosis was good, the doctors said. With luck and time, Katie should recover. Marly clung to those words, refusing to consider any other outcome. She couldn't imagine a life without Katie. She couldn't stand that kind of pain.

Still, it was too early to be certain the treatments had succeeded.

Which was the reason she was back in Dreyerville, sitting in front of the little house she had run away from all those years ago.

After what Katie had suffered, the child deserved her most fervent wish: to meet her grandmother, Winifred Maddox, Marly's mother, one of the few relatives Katie still had. Burly's mother, already an older woman when she had borne her only child, had died four years ago. Mrs. Hanson had no use for children other than her son, and Katie had only seen her once.

Grandmother Hanson was dead, and Burly and his good-for-nothing father were both in the wind. Marly had no idea where Burly had gone when he abandoned them, and she didn't care. Burly had served his purpose and saved her. She had escaped her life in Dreyerville and started on a new path that held far more promise.

Distant memories surfaced, the trip east to Detroit, Burly landing a job as a trucker and Marly starting night classes. It took a while, since she was working as a waitress to help pay the rent, but eventually she had gotten her GED. By then she was eighteen and handling her new life fairly well—until she had gotten pregnant.

The thought stirred a faint thread of anger. A baby was the last thing Burly had wanted—as he'd told her in no uncertain terms. The bigger her belly grew, the later he came home. He took long-haul jobs that kept him away for weeks, and she knew he had begun to see other women. When she came home from night school early, found a pair of red panties on the living room floor and a woman in the bed she and Burly shared, the relationship came crashing to an end.

Marly divorced Burly—which wasn't difficult, since she had never really loved him—and surprised herself by discovering how capable she was. With her job as a waitress, she managed to take care of her newborn baby without Burly's income, then put herself through two years of college. A student loan took care of the next two years. With a small grant and a lot of hard work, she had finally graduated with a teaching credential. For a while, she had worked as a substitute teacher, waiting for a chance at a full-time job.

Then Katie had been diagnosed with cancer.

Marly looked up at the old wooden house. For a moment, she just sat there trying to work up the courage to get out of the car, to march across the uneven sidewalk and climb the front porch steps. She tried to imagine knocking on the front door, tried to guess the greeting she would receive.

Her mother knew they were coming. Winnie had cried when Marly had phoned after so many years. Only a few words were exchanged, just the information that Katie was recovering from cancer and that the child's dearest wish was to meet her grandmother.

Winnie had simply said, "Yes. Oh, yes, please do come home."

The memory of her mother's voice on the phone made her chest feel tight. Older, but still as familiar as it had been when Marly was sixteen.

Her father was dead now. Over the years, she had kept in touch with a few of her friends, and one of them, a girl from Dreyerville High, had written to tell her that Virgil Maddox had passed away. Marly didn't send a sympathy card.

The inside of the Ford was beginning to feel airless and warm. Reaching over, she gently shook Katie's shoulder and the little girl came slowly awake, blinking her big blue eyes as she straightened in her seat.

"Are we there yet?"

Marly smiled at the phrase she had heard a dozen times along the road. "Yes, sweetie, we are."

Katie stretched and yawned, reached for the soft pink knit cap she had been wearing, and pulled it on over her shiny bald head. The doctors had promised the hair would grow back, and though Katie had suffered the indignity of her baldness fairly well, she was still self-conscious. And she had always been shy.

"So are you ready?" Marly asked.

Katie nodded, but her small hand shook as she reached for the door handle. She was a pretty little girl, tall like her mother, blond when she'd had hair, with the same blue eyes as Marly's, the same heart-shaped face. Their features were similar, except that at twenty-eight, Marly bore tiny creases from the corners of her eyes, and she was beginning to see a line or two across her forehead.

She took a courage-building breath, opened the door, and stepped out on her side of the car. Rounding the vehicle to Katie's side, she helped her daughter climb out. They linked arms as they started up the sidewalk that cut across the lawn, which was a little too long and in need of mowing, but now brilliantly green after the end of the cold Michigan winter.

The front door opened before they reached it, and a gray-haired woman Marly almost didn't recognize stepped out onto the porch.

Her mother's lips trembled. "Marly? Oh, dear God, it's really you."

For an instant, Marly stood frozen. Time seemed to spin backward. For an instant, her mother was no longer wrinkled and gray and a little overweight. She was young and lovely with a stunning figure and laughter in her eyes. Drawn by the spell, when her mother reached out, Marly went into her arms and simply hung on.

For long moments, neither of them moved. It felt so good to be there, so good to be surrounded again by her mother's love. Both of them were trembling. The thick lump in Marly's throat made it difficult to swallow.

Another moment lapsed before the ugliness of the past began to intrude. Old memories rose up, bitter and dark. Memories that had her pulling away. Her mother wiped tears from her cheeks with the tips of her fingers and managed to smile.

Marly worked to find her voice. "Mother, this is Katie, your granddaughter. Katie, this is your grandmother Maddox."

Katie smiled shyly. Marly could read the joy in her little girl's face. "Hello . . . Grandma."

More tears filled Winnie's eyes. "Hello, dear heart. I am so happy to meet you."

Katie reached up and self-consciously straightened her cap. "I usually look better. I lost all my hair, but the doctors say it's going to grow back."

Winnie enveloped her in the same warm hug she had given to Marly. "You look beautiful, sweetheart, just the way you are." She managed a watery smile. "You're as pretty as your mother."

Unconsciously, Marly stepped backward. They had been so close once. But things had happened. Things she couldn't forgive.

"Let's get your clothes out of the car," Winnie said to her. "I've got your old room ready. There's a set of twin beds in there, remember? I hope that'll be all right."

Her stomach tightened. Staying in her old room was one of the things she dreaded. There were memories locked up in there. Memories too painful to recall.

She turned toward the street, saw her mother and Katie hauling suitcases out of the trunk of the car, and hurried to join them. Her mother and Katie rolled the overnight bags toward the house while Marly carried the hanging bag the two of them were sharing.

"It's right this way," Winnie said to Katie as they stepped into the living room.

The room looked the same and yet different. The old brown sofa and chair had been covered with a blue floral throw. Plump, light-blue pillows brightened the sofa, and a blue-and-brown fringed paisley rug had been placed beneath the maple coffee table. The brass lamps were the same, but the shade that had been broken during one of her father's rages had been replaced.

She glanced toward the kitchen, saw freshly ironed, light-blue ruffled curtains at the windows. The blinds her father had mostly kept closed were gone, the windows now letting in the late-April sunlight. The old Formica-topped chrome kitchen table remained, but there was a merry little blue-and-white silk flower arrangement in the middle.

"It looks good, Mother . . . what you've done. It looks very nice."

Her mother beamed. She was still pretty, Marly saw, just older and grayer and more weary.

"I gave it a lot of thought," Winnie said. "After your father died, I wanted something cheerful."

Silence fell. The invisible monster in the room had just reared its ugly head. A big, heavyset, beefy man, Virgil Maddox had dominated every inch of the house. There was no place to hide, no way to escape.

In the silence, his presence slowly faded.

"Well, you did a good job, Mother." Not *Mom*, as she used to call her. Somehow the word was too friendly, too intimate for the relationship they now shared.

Her mother glanced away. Perhaps Winnie had caught the flash of remembered pain in Marly's eyes, a reminder of the betrayal that stood between them.

"Come on, Katie." Winnie reached down and took hold of the little girl's hand. "I'll show you where you and your mother will be sleeping."

Katie grabbed the handle of her rolling bag and fell in behind the older woman. As Marly watched them walk away, she noticed a similarity in the way the two of them moved.

Except for the faint limp her mother carried that would never go away.

Her father had been in one of his tempers that day, and her mother had displeased him. She had broken the yolk on one of his eggs, Marly recalled. The fight that resulted had left Winnie with a broken leg and Marly with a broken heart.

She steeled herself, shook the memory away.

When she stood in the hallway and looked into the bedroom, her mother was showing Katie some of the trophies Marly had won when she had been on the Dreyerville High School tennis team. Her father had said tennis was for rich kids, but for once, she had managed to change his mind. She had a knack for the game, she had discovered, and in her sophomore year had won the girls' singles competition.

Unfortunately, by the time she was a junior, things had deteriorated so badly at home that she had dropped off the team and, later that year, dropped out of school.

Marly paused just inside the doorway, unable to take the final steps that would carry her into the bedroom. Inside, nothing had changed. The twin beds were still covered with the same pink quilted bedspreads and matching ruffled throw pillows that had been there when she had lived at home. The nightstands and dresser that she and her mother had painted white, very stylish at the time, were still there, along with the white-painted headboards.

She watched her mother proudly show Katie the framed high school report cards Marly had received, a string of straight As. Her honor roll certificates hung beside them, and her old grammar school science project sat on the dresser: a Styrofoam sun painted yellow surrounded by circles showing the orbit of each perfectly proportioned planet that rotated around it. She had gotten an A on that, too.

Her tennis racquet was missing from its usual spot, she noticed, then remembered that her father had smashed it against the wall in a fit of temper.

As Marly surveyed the interior of the room, a wave of nausea hit her. So much had happened, so many terrible nights spent there, lying in bed listening, waiting for her father to come home. Trying to block out the shouting and crying once he had.

Waiting for another awful night to end.

~2~

In the early-morning hours after Marly and Katie's arrival, it rained, just a light sprinkling that cleared the air, a perfect little storm that left the day sunny and clear.

Winnie Maddox sat at the kitchen table that afternoon, staring out at the garden and thinking it was time to plant. It was strange having Marly home again after so many years. It was strange and wonderful to have her darling granddaughter there in the house.

Oh, the little girl was precious. She reminded Winnie so much of Marly it made her heart hurt. They were both tall and slender, with those pretty blue eyes that had come from Marly's father. Not Marly's no-good husband, Burly, who'd had blue eyes, too. His were pale, and he wasn't handsome the way Virgil had been. With a father as good-looking as Virgil, of course Marly and Katie would be beautiful girls.

They were smart like Virgil, too. She had only known Katie a short time, but it was clear the child was intelligent. And Marly had been an honor student.

Winnie's hand shook as she lifted her coffee cup and took a sip. Because of Virgil, Marly had dropped out of school. She couldn't stand to see her parents fighting or watch the physical assaults Winnie had been forced to suffer.

Still, Marly had made it, done far better than just survived. She had gotten her GED and put herself through college. Winnie had kept up with the events of her daughter's life as best she could through Peggy Ellis, one of Marly's friends from high school. Winnie had never doubted that her daughter would succeed. She was strong and spirited and determined. Marly didn't need anyone but herself.

It was Virgil who had needed Winnie. And because she knew his secrets, she could not leave him.

Marly pulled open the front door just then and walked into the living room carrying two brown paper sacks.

"I went down to King's super and bought us some groceries. A few things Katie especially likes. Cheerios and chocolate milk, some Ruffles potato chips. I figured we'd use them up while we were here."

"I'm making stew for supper," Winnie said brightly. "It was always one of your favorites. I'm planning on baking biscuits, too."

Marly paused in the middle of emptying the second bag. She glanced at the stove, noticed the rich aroma of simmering meat and vegetables that permeated the air, and managed a smile that looked far from sincere.

"It smells wonderful. I'm sure Katie will love it."

Winnie frowned. "What about you?"

"I need to spend some time at the library. I've got a full-time teaching job that starts in September. Chrysler Elementary is one of the top-rated public schools in the Detroit area. I want to bone up on a couple of subjects I'll be teaching in the fall."

"I see." And unfortunately, Winnie saw perfectly. "What you're saying is that you're giving Katie what she wants—a chance to get to know her grandmother. But you don't want to spend time with me yourself."

"I didn't say that."

"It's true, though, isn't it?"

A muscle tightened in Marly's cheek. "I left here twelve years ago, Mother. I never planned to come back. You know the reason I went away. You stayed with a man who beat you rather than divorce him so that we could have some kind of normal life. I was your daughter. Dad ruined my life because you chose his side over mine. It wasn't right then, and just because the years have passed doesn't make it right now."

"I tried to explain. You didn't want to listen to—"

"I know why you stayed. You were in love with him.

You let him ruin your life and mine because you couldn't control your sick feelings for him."

Winnie swallowed and looked away. Marly was right, at least in part. In the beginning, she had loved Virgil Maddox with every ounce of her soul, but there was far more to the story than that. Unfortunately, even after all these years, she didn't think her daughter was ready to hear it.

"I'll get something at the drive-through," Marly said. "Tell Katie not to wait up for me."

And then she was gone.

Winnie sank back down in her chair, her gaze fixed on the place her daughter had been. Her heart was aching, hurting the way it had during the weeks after Marly had left. The note Winnie had found on the bed hadn't made it any easier.

I'm gone, Mom. I'm marrying Burly, so you don't have to worry. It was signed simply, *Marly.*

The ache expanded. Marrying a no-account like Burly Hanson was the last thing she had wanted for her beautiful, intelligent daughter.

Winnie had made a mistake. She should have known something would happen, should have done something before it was too late.

But twelve years was a long time, and everything was

different now. Virgil was dead and Burly was gone and there was little Katie to consider.

Winnie sat there thinking of Katie and how much the little girl already meant to her. She wanted to see her granddaughter again, wanted to spend time with both of her girls. What could she say that could mend the rift between her and Marly? How could she make her daughter understand?

How could she possibly gain Marly's forgiveness for the things she should have done?

Katie wandered around the backyard of her grandmother's old gray house. In Detroit they lived in a four-unit apartment building. It wasn't fancy, but it was okay. The city was fun in some ways. She could skateboard on the sidewalk, and there were ice-cream stores and movie theaters right around the block. But car horns blared all the time and people yelled at each other.

And they didn't have a nice big yard like this. Some of her grandma's spring flowers were already up and blooming. The weather wasn't as cold as it had been, and warm sunshine pushed through the few fluffy clouds in the sky. An old wooden fence surrounded the yard, in the center of which grew a big hickory tree, its branches flaring out over the long, green grass.

Katie walked over and peered between the boards in the fence, into the yard of the house next door. It seemed about as old as Grandma's, only it was two stories high and looked a lot better. A fresh coat of slate-blue paint covered the wooden siding, and the white shutters looked newly painted. The yard was well kept and all the shrubs neatly trimmed.

A pair of ice skates hung from one of the posts that held up the porch, and a red Flexible Flyer sled sat next to a skateboard against the wall.

Katie moved a little, peered through another crack to view the house from a different angle, wondering who lived there and making up imaginary people. A kindly old man and his grandson, a couple with a newborn baby, a handsome man who needed a wife and wanted to be a father.

She laughed at this last thought, kind of a silly secret wish, then shrieked and jumped back as a big, black-and-tan, scruffy-looking dog with stiff, curly hair barked and lunged at the fence. She stood there shaking, angry at herself for not realizing the dog was in the yard, yet curious to get a better look at him.

She got a closer look than she planned when the dog jumped over a low spot in the fence at the back of the yard and ran toward her. She might have been frightened if it weren't for the sappy look on the mutt's homely face.

He stopped right in front of her and cocked his silly-looking head.

Katie laughed. "Hey, boy, what's your name?"

Clearly he wasn't a biter, for he nudged her hand, trying to get her to pet him. And he wasn't as big as she'd thought, just a medium-sized dog with those little ears that stuck up and flopped over at the top, a terrier of some kind, she figured, since her friend, Cindy, had a dog that looked a little like it.

"You won't bite me, will you?" Tentatively she reached toward him.

"He won't bite," came a boy's voice from a few feet away. He was hanging over the fence, wearing a dirt-smudged navy-blue sweatshirt and jeans. "His name's Rufus." He was a good-looking boy, maybe a year or two older than she was, with dark brown hair and brown eyes.

Unconsciously, she reached up to her pink knit cap, saw his gaze follow the movement, and jerked her hand away in embarrassment.

"I had cancer," she said, because she knew he wouldn't ask, just stare at her and wonder what had happened to make her bald. "My hair fell out, but it's supposed to grow back."

"Wow. Cancer. So are you okay?"

She shrugged. "I hope so. The doctors think I'll get well."

"That's good." He hopped over the fence with an ease that said he was good at sports. But she could have figured that from the stuff on his porch.

"Was it terrible?" he asked. "The treatment, I mean. I heard it makes you really sick."

She didn't like to think of the bouts of nausea, and throwing up everything she'd eaten, or the way her hair had come out in frightening handfuls. "It was awful."

"But it's over, right?"

She just nodded. He was even better-looking up close, the kind of boy who used to pay attention to her but hadn't since she got sick. "I missed a lot of school. My mom's a teacher. She's going to help me get caught up."

"My name's Hamilton. Everyone calls me Ham."

"Ham. That's cool. I'm Katie. My mom brought me here to meet my grandmother. Probably in case I end up dying."

"You're gonna get well," Ham said firmly. "I can tell by looking at you. You look really healthy."

She brightened. "Thanks."

"Mrs. Maddox is super nice. Whenever she bakes cookies, she brings some over for my dad and me."

"What about your mom?"

He shrugged. "She died four years ago. It's just me and my dad now."

"You must miss her."

He glanced away. "Yeah."

Katie reached down and picked up a dry hickory branch, twirled it in her hand. "My dad ran off when I was a baby. I don't even know what he looks like."

"That's rough."

"I guess so. Mom said her dad was so mean she wished he would have run off and left her."

Ham looked back toward his house. "My dad's cool. He's a sheriff."

"A sheriff? You mean like a policeman?"

He nodded. "You'll have to come over and meet him sometime. How long are you staying?"

"I don't know. A week or two. My mom and my grandma don't get along very well." She couldn't figure out why she was telling him all this stuff. Ham just . . . well, he was being so nice to her. And it felt good to talk to a boy again. Most of them felt funny around her now.

He reached down and ruffled his dog's curly black-and-tan coat. "Listen, I gotta go. Tomorrow's Saturday. You want to come over and play some Ping-Pong? We got a table set up on the sunporch. My dad'll be home unless he gets a call and has to leave."

"Sure, that sounds like fun."

"How about late morning? I've got some chores to do first, then we can play."

"Okay."

He tugged playfully on his dog's bent ear. "Come on, Ruf, let's go." Boy and dog headed for the fence. Ham went over first and Rufus made a leap behind him. His hand went up above the fence in a final wave, and then he ran for the back door of the house.

As Katie watched him disappear, a lump formed in her throat. She felt like crying, though she didn't quite know why. She had made a new friend, and lately, it hadn't been that easy.

Thinking of Ham, she brightened. Turning, she raced off to tell her grandmother the exciting news.

~3~

Reed Bennett checked his appearance in the mirror. His dark hair was combed, his beige uniform nicely tailored and neatly pressed. He rubbed a thumb across his jaw, satisfied with his morning shave. His fly was zipped, so he was ready to go.

He almost smiled. His son had made a new friend and invited her over to play Ping-Pong later this morning. When Ham had told him the girl was recovering from cancer, Reed's heart went out to both Katie and her family. He was proud of his son for taking such a bold step, and he wanted to reassure the girl's mother and Mrs. Maddox that Katie was welcome and that he would watch out for her while she was in his home.

He was ready to go next door, but it was early yet and he had an errand to run.

"I'll be back in an hour," he called to Ham, who was busy cleaning his room. "I need to stop by the office. Just remember, Mrs. Maddox is right next door if something happens."

Winnie Maddox was a wonderful neighbor. She had volunteered to keep an eye on Ham, who, having just turned twelve, was finally old enough to stay home alone. She was always bringing over cakes and cookies, and left-over bones for Rufus.

Reed continued out the door, climbed into his sheriff's car, and started the engine. It was Dreyervill County policy for deputies to take their cars home with them after they got off duty. Having a patrol car parked in the neighborhood had proven to be a great deterrent to crime.

Reed pulled away from the house and drove toward his destination. Technically he was off on weekends, but he had a couple of things to check on at the office and he preferred to go in uniform in case something came up.

He pulled into King's Supermarket, picked up a gallon of milk and some raspberry strudel, then got back in his car and headed across town.

On Main Street, he waved at a skinny kid named Freddie, a friend of Ham's, and made the slow-down sign to a teenager named Joey Ekstrom who was driving over the speed limit—not for the first time. Turning onto Alder, he pulled up in front of a yellow ranch-style home with a slightly tilted mailbox in front.

Reed made a mental note to fix it. The yard needed some care as well, and he reminded himself to stop by after work one day next week and get it done.

Climbing out of the car, he carried the groceries up to the door and knocked. Emily Carter, a petite young woman with short dark hair and a turned-up nose, smiled at him and opened the door a little wider.

"Reed! Come on in. I was just pouring myself a cup of coffee. How about I pour you one, too?"

"Sure." He walked inside and Emily closed the door. Aside from a few stuffed animals sitting neatly in an over-stuffed chair and a plastic tricycle parked against the wall, the house was spotlessly clean—almost too clean.

"Timmy isn't up yet," Emily said. "Let me get you that coffee."

"Sounds good." He handed her the milk and raspberry strudel. "I brought you these. I figured you could use them."

She carried the bag to the kitchen counter, looked inside. "Great. Thanks."

Emily wasn't surprised to see him, he knew. Reed had been stopping by the house on a regular basis for the last six months. He'd been doing so ever since Deputy Randall Carter had died in the line of duty six months ago while making a routine traffic stop. When a drunk driver had swerved into his patrol car, Randy had been killed instantly, leaving behind his wife and three-year-old son.

Reed knew what it felt like to lose a loved one. He still missed Carol every day. He knew how lonely Emily must be, how hard it was for her to get through each day, so he and some of the other guys in the department made it a point to stop by as often as they could. They helped with the household chores Randy used to do and anything else Emily might need.

She poured coffee into a couple of mugs, cut each of them a slice of strudel, and carried them over to the small oak table in the kitchen. The counter was as clean and tidy as the rest of the house. Reed was sure she must be working long hours at home to keep her mind off Randy.

They talked about the weather, about Timmy's recovery from a recent cold. They had known each other since high school, since before Reed had left for college to get his degree in police science. Before he'd become the county sheriff. Before Emily had married Randy.

It seemed as if they had always been friends. But it was Carol whom Reed had fallen in love with. Though the pain of her death was beginning to lessen, the agony of grief beginning to soften and fade, he would never be able to forget her or the life they had shared.

Reed took a last drink of coffee, got up, and carried his empty plate and mug over to the sink.

"I'm afraid I have to go, Em. I've got to stop by the office, and Ham's got a friend coming over. I need to get my work done and head back home."

"I'm sure you have lots to do." She looked disappointed, but she always did when he left. He imagined she liked having someone other than her little boy to talk to, to help keep her mind off Randy. Until her husband's death, she had worked as a clerk at Suzy's, a little Main Street boutique that sold women's clothes. She hadn't gone back to work and now just lived on Randy's modest pension.

"Thanks for the milk," she said as she walked him to the door. "You always seem to know what we need."

He smiled. "When does a mother raising a little boy not need a gallon of milk?"

She laughed. "You're right. Tell Ham hello for me."

"I will." He was reaching for the door knob when he heard the muffled sound of running feet and looked up to see Timmy racing toward him in a pair of footed pajamas with miniature owls on them.

"Uncle Weed!" the little boy shouted, his tiny elbows pumping as he ran for all he was worth. Reed went down on one knee, caught the boy in his arms, and lifted him high into the air.

Timmy giggled and laughed, and Reed set the child back on his feet.

"What'd you bwing me, Uncle Weed?"

"I brought you some raspberry strudel. I had a piece myself and it was really good."

"I love it." He turned to his mother. "I'm hungry, Mama. Can I have some?"

Emily smiled. "I think we can manage that." She lifted him up, propped him against her shoulder. "Your Uncle Reed has to leave. Tell him good-bye."

"Bye, Uncle Weed."

Reed chuckled, reached over, and ruffled the boy's light brown hair. "Bye, Timmy. Take care of yourself, Em."

She smiled as she carried her son into the kitchen. Reed let himself out, closed the door behind him, made sure it was locked, and returned to his car.

From Emily's he drove straight to the Dreyerville County Sheriff's Office a few miles outside town. Eager to get his work done and be on his way back home, he parked the car and went inside.

"Hey, Sheriff, you forget it's Saturday?" It was Millie Caswell, the indispensible woman who ran the office. In her mid-forties, with medium-brown hair beginning to gray, Millie was happily married and the mother-hen type who looked out for every deputy in the department.

"I've just got a couple of things to check," he said, "then I'm out of here."

"You'd better be. You know how Ham looks forward to your weekends together."

"Ham's got a Ping-Pong date this morning. I've got to get back and play chaperone." Which reminded him that as soon as he got there, he needed to go over and speak to Winnie's daughter. Her name was Marly, he knew, and he wondered what she would be like.

Winnie talked about her often, but always in the past tense as if she were dead: Marly was really good at tennis. Marly got straight As when she was in school. Marly always wanted a puppy.

He knew that the pair had had a serious falling-out. Marly had run off and married one of the locals, and Winnie hadn't seen her since. He wasn't sure about her marital status now, but surely it was past time for the rift between mother and daughter to be healed.

Reed hoped so. He knew it would make Winnie happy.

He made a few phone calls, checked on the status of a burglary that had taken place in a house out on the lake, and said good-bye to Millie.

Sliding behind the wheel of his patrol car, he fired up the big V-8 engine, and headed for home, thinking of his son and the little girl from next door, curious about the woman who had fled Dreyerville some twelve years ago.

~4~

Marly watched the sheriff's car pull into the driveway of the house next door, which sat on a much larger lot than her mother's small home. She remembered that the Cassidy family used to live there and wondered if they still did. Her gaze went back out the window. She had noticed the car as it was leaving and she hoped nothing was wrong.

"What is it?" her mother asked, walking up to peer over her shoulder.

"What's the sheriff doing at the Cassidy house?"

Winnie waved her hand. "Oh, that's nothing to worry about. Sheriff Bennett lives there now. His wife died a few years back. It's just him and his boy, Hamilton. Ham, they call him. Ham invited Katie over to play Ping-Pong this morning. She was really excited about it. She wanted to tell you, but you were still at the library when she went to bed."

She had stayed out late on purpose. She had promised to give Winnie time with Katie. And being out of the house kept her own demons at bay.

Just then Katie wandered out of the bedroom into the kitchen. She had showered and dressed for the day in jeans and a pink T-shirt with a glittery flower on the front. She perked up when she saw Marly.

"Hey, Mom, guess what? Yesterday, I met this really neat boy. His name's Ham and he lives next door and he invited me over to play Ping-Pong. Can I go, Mom? Please?"

Marly hadn't seen that glow on her daughter's face in weeks. She looked back out the window, saw a tall, dark-haired man in a beige uniform get out of the white, brown-striped sheriff's car. Instead of going into his own home, he turned and crossed the lawn, walking toward Winnie's porch.

"The sheriff . . ." Marly said. "He's coming over here."

"Good," Winnie said. "You'll get to meet him."

Katie dashed to the window. "He must be Ham's dad. He looks just like Ham, only a whole lot bigger."

Winnie hustled from the kitchen into the living room and opened the door at the first light knock.

"Come on in, Sheriff," Winnie said. "We were just talking about you. We saw you drive up." She turned. "This is my daughter, Marly Hanson. And this is my granddaughter, Katie."

Marly managed to smile. "It's nice to meet you, Sheriff Bennett."

His return smile was wide and warm. "Since we're neighbors, I'd rather you just called me Reed." His gaze flicked to Katie in her pink T-shirt, pink knit cap, and jeans. "It's nice to meet you, both."

The sheriff was a handsome man, Marly noticed, with his dark hair, strong jaw, and clear brown eyes. Not that it mattered all that much. She had learned a long time ago, it was what was inside a man that counted.

"Katie says Ham invited her over to play Ping-Pong," Winnie said to Reed. "He mention that to you?"

"As a matter of fact, that's the reason I'm here. I wanted to make sure you knew it was okay with me and that I would be there to chaperone. If I get a call and have to leave, I'll send her home."

"Is it all right, Mom?" Katie pleaded. "Please say yes."

Marly's smile was more sincere. "Why not? What better chaperone than a sheriff?"

"Yippee!" Katie whirled around, one hand holding her hat in place so it wouldn't fly off and reveal her bald head. Marly's heart squeezed.

"Can I go over now?" Katie asked.

"You can go whenever the sheriff says."

"Give me a minute and I'll walk you over myself," he said.

Katie beamed, turned, and raced out onto the porch.

"It was nice of your son to invite her," Marly said to Reed. "She's had a very tough year."

"Ham told me about the cancer. It couldn't have been easy on either of you."

Something softened inside her. That he might understand the agony she had been through, the heartbreaking worry, made her take a second look at him. Maybe there was more to Reed Bennett than just a pretty face. "No, it wasn't."

He nodded, started for the door, hesitated a moment, and turned back. "Maybe the three of you would like to come over for a barbeque one night. And your husband, of course, if he's here."

"I don't have a husband. Haven't for a very long time."

He smiled. He had a dynamite smile. "The three of you, then. I make great barbecued chicken."

"I could bake us a cake," Winnie added, excitement in her voice.

Marly looked at her mother's expectant face and wanted to say no. She would be leaving by the end of next week at the latest—the sooner the better, as far as she was concerned. She was only there for Katie. She didn't want to spend more time with her mother than she absolutely had to. She didn't want all the bad memories crawling up from inside her.

Katie ran back through the open front door. "Can we, Mom?" Obviously she had been listening. "We never get to do anything like that."

Katie was looking at her with those pleading blue eyes. Winnie was looking at her with hope. How could she not say yes?

She turned to Reed. "All right. What night?"

"How about tomorrow?"

"That's Sunday. Okay, that should be fine."

"So we'll see you at church," Winnie said brightly. "Then later, we'll come over for supper."

"Sounds good," Reed said.

But Marly was thinking that she hadn't been to church since she had left Dreyerville. Surely her mother didn't expect her to go.

"We'll see you tomorrow," Reed said, casting Marly a glance that was a little more male than she had expected. He waited for Katie to scamper back out onto the porch, and then he quietly closed the door behind them.

Marly sank down in one of the chrome kitchen chairs. Just working up the courage to come back had been unbelievably stressful. Now she was going with her mother and daughter to a barbecue at the neighbors' house.

"He liked you," Winnie said, smiling. "I could tell."

"He was just being polite. He's a sheriff. He's supposed to be polite."

Winnie opened one of the cupboards and took down a mixing bowl. "I think I'll get started on that cake. It'll hold till tomorrow. You want to help? You used to love helping me bake."

Marly's temper sparked. She shot up from the chair, her patience at an end. "I was a kid, Mother. I stopped helping you bake when Dad came home drunk and beat the crap out of you."

Winnie's face fell.

"I'm going to the library. I'll see you later."

Her mother said nothing, just watched as Marly disappeared out the door.

Timmy yawned. The early afternoon sun poured through the windows, warming the living room and making the little boy's eyes begin to droop. He sat on the floor with a crayon in his hand and his coloring book open, trying to figure out what shade of blue to make a tree.

"Mama, will you color with me?"

Emily reached down and picked him up, propped him on her hip. She had been doing housework all morning, and he seemed to weigh more than he usually did.

"Tell you what, sport. After you have your nap, we'll color. How about that?"

For once he didn't argue. His small body sagged sleepily against her, and she kissed the top of his head.

"Okay . . . ," he said, his head drooping against her shoulder. He'd been playing with his Hot Wheels all morning, toys one of the deputies had gotten at McDonald's and brought over for him. He had more energy than the average three-year-old, but when he ran out of steam, he collapsed like a pin-pricked balloon.

She carried him into his bedroom and put him down for his nap, waited for a moment to be sure he was asleep, then quietly closed the door, leaving it open a crack.

She had a little time, enough to get a few more chores done. Carrying in the rickety old wooden ladder she had found in the garage, she set it up in the kitchen, grabbed a wet rag, and climbed the rungs.

The ladder wiggled a little, reminding her to be careful but not worrying her enough to stop. She needed to reach the shelf above the kitchen counter. She needed to dust it again.

Emily moved the silk plants and baskets that decorated the shelf, wiped off whatever dust might have accumulated in less than a week, took the rag and began to scrub a spot she had missed when she had dusted last week. She had already mopped and vacuumed and washed the living room windows, which were spotted from the light rain that had fallen a few days ago. She would do the rest tomorrow.

She scrubbed hard on the spot. She was almost finished when the doorbell rang. She glanced toward the front door, for an instant thinking it might be Reed. Probably not, since he had been there just that morning. She always looked forward to his visits. In high school, she'd had a crush on him, but once he'd met Carol, he had never really noticed her again.

With a sigh, she climbed down the ladder. Tossing the wet rag into the sink, she wiped her hands on her apron and crossed the living room. For an instant, when she spotted the uniform through the window, she thought she was wrong and Reed had returned, but when she pulled open the door, another officer stood on the porch.

"Hello, Emily."

She stepped back, letting Deputy Patrick Murphy walk past her into the living room. "Hi, Pat."

He took off his brown felt hat and held it in both hands. "I . . . ummm . . . thought I'd stop by . . . see if there was anything you might need." He had brownish red hair and hazel eyes. He had a nice smile, though he was a little bit shy about using it.

She tried to smile in return, but all of a sudden, she felt exhausted and wound up just shaking her head. "The sheriff was here this morning. He brought me some milk. That's all I really needed."

Patrick turned his hat brim in his big, lightly freckled hands. He was a year younger than she was. She knew because he had also gone to Dreyerville High.

"I . . . ummm . . . noticed your yard needs some work. With winter over, the shrubs are growing like crazy. The bushes could use a trim, get spruced up a bit. Be nice to put in some spring flowers."

She glanced out the window. "I've been so busy with the house I . . . I hadn't thought about the yard. I'll have to get out there this week."

He blanched. "I didn't mean for you to do it. I was thinking . . . you know, maybe I'd stop by and do it for you."

"That isn't necessary, Patrick."

"I'd like to help, Em. I mean . . . if you wouldn't mind."

She released a shaky breath. "That's very nice of you, Pat, but—"

"I could start tomorrow. My shift ends at three. It would only take me a couple of days."

He was trying to help. Everyone had been so nice since Randy died. It made her guilt even worse.

"That's really kind of you . . . if you're sure you wouldn't mind."

Patrick smiled. "I wouldn't mind at all." He was a nice-looking man, she thought. Even the slightly crooked nose he had gotten in a fist fight in high school didn't detract from his appearance. She wondered why he wasn't married.

"I'll be here tomorrow after my shift is over. I left my phone number the last time I was here. You still have it, right?"

If she did, she had no idea where it was. "I'm sure I do." And she could probably find it. Before Randy died, she had been so disorganized. It was one of the things he disliked about her, but she was better about it now.

"If you need anything, just call and I'll pick it up on my way over."

She nodded, gave him a weary smile. "Thank you, Patrick."

"I'll see you tomorrow, then."

She walked him to the door, watched him through the window as he made his way along the cement walkway. The car door opened and he slid behind the wheel. The engine roared to life. He backed out of the driveway and drove away.

The deputies who continued to stop by were all

friends of Randy's. They all felt sorry for her because her husband had been killed.

She wondered if they would still want to help if they knew he'd been planning to leave her, that as far as Randy was concerned, their marriage was over. He didn't love her anymore, he had said. She was a terrible wife and mother, and he was leaving her for someone else. How he had managed to keep it a secret, she would never know. Maybe the woman was married. Emily still had no idea who the woman was and didn't want to know.

All she knew was that Randy had told her he wanted a divorce and he was taking Timmy with him when he left.

He had made the announcement just hours before he had been killed.

As she thought of that day, guilt expanded inside her. She should have loved him more. She should have been a better wife, better mother. She should have kept the house cleaner, learned to be a better cook.

She shouldn't have felt that instant of relief when he said he was leaving.

She wondered what would happen if the deputies found out her secret, wondered if they would abandon her, the way her husband had planned to do. Her chest felt tight the way it did sometimes when she thought about Randy.

She looked up to see Timmy racing into the room. Surely it hadn't been an hour yet. Surely it wasn't time for his nap to be over. But there he was running toward her, his baggy jeans flapping, his T-shirt flattened against his narrow little boy's chest. He grinned as he crossed the room.

"Can we color now?" He had Randy's same brown eyes, same light brown hair. But in most ways, she thought he was more like her than his father.

She knelt in front of him with open arms, and he ran in for a hug. She loved him so much. The cleaning could wait until later. Her son was more important.

"Get your coloring book and put it up on the coffee table."

"I'll get it!" He raced over to where he had left it on the floor.

Randy had said she was a bad mother. That she left Timmy with a sitter too often, that she should have quit her job and stayed home to take care of them both.

She didn't work anymore. She just stayed home and took care of her boy.

Sometimes she thought she would go crazy.

Reed stood at the door leading into the sunroom, where a fierce Ping-Pong tournament was still taking place. The kids had been playing for hours and were surprisingly well matched. Ham usually beat most of the kids in the neighborhood, but Katie was holding her own.

She slammed the white ball down, Ham missed the return, and she let out a peal of laughter. Ham laughed good-naturedly in return.

Reed couldn't help but smile. Katie was a sweet little girl. If Carol had lived, they might have had more children. After Ham was born, both of them had wanted to try for a girl, but Carol miscarried two times in a row and the doctor thought it would be unwise to try again too soon.

The years slipped past. They were considering another attempt or possibly adopting a baby when Carol had been killed.

A chill slid through him. It had been raining that night, the wind blowing up a gale. Carol had been returning from a visit with her mother, who lived in the next county over. The roads were slick and the curve wasn't banked quite right. Neither driver was held responsible. Something just went wrong.

Fate took Carol that dark night four years ago, and part of Reed just shut down. Ham had only been eight at the time. The boy had finally recovered from the devastating loss of his mother, accepting his circumstances and moving forward again.

Reed wished he had progressed as fast as his son. It had only been lately that he had begun to think of more than work and Ham, more about himself and what he wanted out of life.

Which returned this attention to Ham and Katie and the Ping-Pong match being played in front of him. His thoughts strayed from Katie to her mother, who was prettier than he would have guessed.

Winnie was only in her fifties, but she hadn't aged well. Her face was more wrinkled than it should have been, her shoulders already a little stooped. She limped slightly, an old injury of some sort, he guessed.

He wouldn't have expected the daughter to be tall and straight-shouldered, slender, with what appeared, in the snug-fitting jeans she'd been wearing, to be long, very nicely shaped legs.

Winnie's gray hair and hazel eyes hadn't prepared him for the daughter's blue eyes and shiny blond hair. She wore it in a neat French braid, but little wispy curls escaped, making him curious as to what it would look like if she left it unbound.

He hadn't really been attracted to a woman since Carol had died. Hadn't felt that little kick in the gut a man feels when he meets a woman who appeals to all his male instincts. But today, he had actually thought of asking Marly Hanson to go out with him.

He liked Winnie. And Marly's daughter seemed a well-adjusted, well-cared-for child, happy, considering all she had been through. If Marly was anything like either one of them, he might be interested in getting to know her, maybe even taking her out.

But a date was a major step. The barbecue was a compromise. Safer. No pressure on either of them. If they didn't get along, she'd go home and that would be the end of it.

And it was clear Katie would enjoy it.

He watched the kids play and felt a pang because he and Carol hadn't been able to have more children. Maybe it would happen if he ever remarried. It didn't seem possible at the moment, but there was always a chance.

Life had a way of going in directions you didn't expect.

It had already happened to him once; it could happen again.

Reed wasn't sure how he felt about the notion.

Winnie ended up taking Katie to church on Sunday morning while Marly stayed home and worked on some of her lesson plans for the class she would be teaching in Detroit in the fall. Or at least that was what Marly had said.

It made Winnie sad to think that her sins had driven her daughter away not only from her, but also from God.

Sitting in the long mahogany pew, she reached over and squeezed Katie's hand. The child had been quiet throughout the service, the subject of which had been forgiveness. Years ago, Winnie had forgiven Marly for running away, for leaving a hole in her heart that still hadn't mended. She just wished her daughter would consider forgiving *her*.

As the service came to a close, the Reverend Gains walked up the aisle and stepped out onto the porch in front of the tall, arched doors to greet his flock as they departed. Winnie urged Katie up from the pew and wandered along with the congregation toward the door.

The church was old and lovely, with an old-fashioned tall, white steeple and stained-glass windows that let in rainbow-colored light. Katie adjusted her knit cap, this one blue to match her Sunday church dress, and they slowed as they reached the minister, who conversed with several members of the church.

He turned, smiled in Winnie's direction. "Hello, Winifred."

"Reverend." He was a tall, heavyset blond man with warm brown eyes and the kind of smile you could trust. "And this must be your granddaughter, Katie. You mentioned she was coming for a visit."

"That's right. Katie, say hello to Reverend Gains."

"Hello, Reverend."

The minister glanced around and Winnie knew he was looking for Marly.

"Mom didn't come," Katie told him. "She said the steeple would probably fall off if she went back to church after all these years."

The reverend just smiled. "I remember your mother. Tell her I said we're willing to take our chances. Tell her my wife and I would both be pleased to see her in church again."

"I'll tell her, but I don't think she'll come."

Winnie led Katie away, glad her granddaughter wasn't as antisocial as Marly had become. Maybe tonight would be better.

She found herself smiling. Her daughter might try to pretend otherwise, but she was still a beautiful young woman and Reed Bennett was an extremely attractive man.

Wouldn't it be wonderful if—

Her chest clamped down as if she were suffering one of her asthma spells. Unless something changed, Marly wouldn't be staying in Dreyerville long enough for something wonderful to happen.

The joy Winnie had been feeling slowly melted away.

The barbecue that evening went smoothly. The weather cooperated by remaining unseasonably warm, and to her dismay, Marly discovered she was actually enjoying herself.

"This chicken is wonderful," she said to Reed, who sat across from her at the picnic table out in his backyard. She licked sweet red barbecue sauce from her fingers. "I'll have to get your recipe."

He chuckled. "My recipe is, purchase a package of chicken that's already cut up, put it on the grill, cook it till it's brown, and slather it with any flavor barbecue sauce you buy at the store." He smiled. "I'm really not much of a cook."

"You did just fine tonight."

He sank his teeth into a drumstick. When he swallowed the bite, he chased it with a swallow of iced tea. "How about you? You like to cook?"

She ran a finger around the rim of her glass. "My mother was the cook in our family. Her meals were delicious."

Reed frowned. "Do you realize you and your mother both talk about each other in the past tense? You're both still alive, you know."

Her lips tightened. "This life died for me a long time ago."

Reed sipped his tea, eyeing her over the rim of the glass. "I can't believe Winnie was that bad a mother."

Marly's gaze swung toward the woman standing in front of the card table cutting into the double-layer chocolate cake she had baked. Next to her, Katie and Ham waited impatiently for her to serve them a slice. The dog, Rufus, sat beside them wagging his tail, hoping for a piece of his own.

"In most ways, Winnie was a wonderful mother. She went to every parent-teacher conference, made sure I had decent clothes, helped me with my homework, always gave me encouragement when I needed it."

"But? . . ."

Marly shrugged, uncomfortable with the direction of

the conversation. "There were other, more important things she didn't do."

"Like? . . ."

She straightened on the bench. "Look, it's really none of your business."

"No, it isn't. Except that I like Winifred Maddox and I'm starting to like you, too. Helping people is part of my job. Helping people I care about feels like the right thing to do."

"You can't help me, Reed. Too much has happened. Too many years have gone by. Too many old hurts that'll never mend."

"If it wasn't your mother," he pressed, "it must have been your dad. What did he do?"

A cold chill swept through her. She looked up at him and shook her head. "You don't give up, do you?"

He smiled. "Not easily. Though in this case, I probably should."

"Why?"

"Because I'd like to ask you out and you won't say yes if I keep interfering in your business."

She laughed. She looked at him and felt a funny little lift in her stomach. He was even better-looking in jeans and a light blue shirt than he had been in his uniform.

"I haven't been out on a date in years," she said. "Not since before Katie got sick. Not often before that."

"Why not?"

"I don't know. Probably because my experiences with men haven't been very good."

"Men like your dad."

"That's right. And my husband."

Her mother walked up just then and handed them each a piece of cake on a paper plate, along with a plastic fork. "I thought about putting chopped nuts on top the way you always liked," she said, "but I didn't know if Katie liked nuts."

"She loves them." Marly looked down at the cake and could almost see the walnuts pressing into the thick chocolate frosting, something special her mother had added just for her. Her eyes swam for an instant before she blinked the image away. It was getting harder and harder to be stoic, to keep her distance the way she had vowed to do. She took a calming breath and slowly released it. "The cake looks great."

Reed took an oversized bite. "It's delicious, Winnie," he said around a mouthful, and her mother beamed.

"I'm glad you like it." Winnie waited impatiently for her daughter to take a bite, then smiled at the look of pleasure Marly couldn't keep from washing into her face.

"It tastes even better than it looks," Marly admitted, but as she had said, her mother had always been a great cook.

Winnie cast her a last soft glance as she walked away.

"She loves you," Reed said. "She talks about you all the time."

"In the past tense."

"As I understand it, you haven't seen each other in years. Until you came back, there hasn't been a present tense."

With nothing to say in reply, she took another bite of the delicious cake. Memories rushed in. She and her mother baking a cake just like this one, the kitchen filled with the aroma of cocoa and vanilla.

Then her dad had driven up in his pickup, opened his door, and fallen out of the truck onto the cement driveway. Winnie had dropped the spoon in her hand and raced out to help him. At least he had waited until he got into the house before he slapped her face.

"What is it?" Reed's voice brought her back to the present. "You all right? You look kind of pale."

A slow breath escaped. "I was thinking of the past. For me, it's never a good thing to do."

"Sometimes dealing with the past is the only way you can move into the future."

Marly took a sip of the frosty iced tea. "My mother told me you lost your wife. Have you been able to deal with that and move into the future?"

He sighed. "I wish I could say I have. I'm trying. It's harder than I thought it would be. Maybe you should at least give it a try."

Marly shook her head. "I've spent the last twelve years trying to forget all of this. Now I'm right back where I started. I can't tell you how happy I'll be to leave."

"When are you going?"

"I promised Katie we'd stay a couple of weeks."

He smiled. "Plenty of time for that date."

Marly looked up at him. Why not? He was a handsome man, one who had other nice qualities as well. Why shouldn't she make the best of a bad situation? "All right. When do you want to go?"

"How about tomorrow? We could all go out for pizza and a movie. Unfortunately, it's a school night for Ham, but Katie's welcome to come with us."

That was something new. A man asking her to go out with him and bring her daughter along.

"She doesn't have much time to spend with her grandmother. It'll have to be just the two of us."

Reed smiled. "I think I can handle that. How's seven o'clock?"

"Sounds good."

They finished the rest of their cake and then began the job of cleaning up. It had been a remarkably enjoyable evening. Worth the tense moments when Reed's questions had pushed her into the painful past.

But the sheriff wasn't the sort to give up. He would want to know more, and he wouldn't quit pressing until he had the answers to his questions.

In a town the size of Dreyerville, it wasn't fair to her mother to divulge long-buried secrets. Long after Marly left, Winnie would be forced to deal with whatever her daughter revealed.

Then again, since Marly had been living with the knowledge for years, maybe it was poetic justice.

~6~

An unexpected storm blew in the first of the week. It rained all night, mostly a light patter on the roof that Winnie always found comforting. The rain had stopped, but the grass was wet this morning, little drops of water glittering in the sunshine that poked through the dissipating clouds.

"What was Grandpa like?"

The question took Winnie completely by surprise. She and Katie were sitting out in the screened-in porch that opened off the washroom, each of them peeling an apple. Winnie had promised to bake a pie if Katie would help her.

A long strand of apple peel fell into the small tin bucket on the table in front of Winnie. "I guess the way your mama feels, you wouldn't know much about him."

Winnie flicked her granddaughter a sideways glance. Katie was wearing her pink knit cap the way she always did. Without hair, her features were more pronounced, the smooth, fair skin, the small, straight nose and bow-shaped lips.

"I've never even seen a picture," Katie said.

"I suppose I could remedy that." Sliding back her chair, Winnie stood up and stepped into the house, returning a few minutes later with a five-by-seven framed photo of her and Virgil on their wedding day. She handed it to Katie, sat down, and started back to work.

"You can see how handsome he was. In his day, he was one of the best-looking men in the county. That's where you and your mama got your pretty blue eyes. From your grandpa Virgil."

Katie studied the picture. "Mom said he was mean."

The apple peeler stilled in Winnie's hand. She took a deep breath and went to peeling again. "There was a time he was a real nice man, your grandpa, back when I first met him. He was a fireman, you know. Worked for the Dreyerville Fire Department. And oh, he loved his job."

"Mom never said he was a fireman."

"Well, he was, and a good one. I was just out of high school when we met. My folks' old clapboard house at the edge of town caught fire, and Virgil and his crew came to the rescue." She smiled, recalling that day and the handsome man who had swept into her bedroom, broken out the window, and helped her climb to safety.

"I fell in love with him right then and there," she said,

"and he must have taken a fancy to me, too, because a year later, we were married."

Katie stood the framed photo up on the table so she could still see it. "Then Mom was born."

"That's right. It didn't happen right away, but a few years after we took our vows, your mother was born and Virgil was so happy. He was a good husband back then."

"Mom says he hit you."

Her chest clamped down. She didn't want to say bad things about Virgil even after all these years. But she wasn't going to lie for him, either.

"Something happened at work. Your grandpa started drinking. He didn't do it that often, but when he did, he got real mean."

"What happened at work?" Katie asked, the apple in her hand long forgotten.

"There was a fire down at Tremont's Antiques. Old Mrs. Tremont was caught upstairs in the third-floor attic. She was too old to jump out the window, so your grandpa went inside to save her. Only thing was, the fire got worse and the attic floor gave way and poor old Mrs. Tremont fell through and got killed."

"But Grandpa got out?"

"Yes, he did, but he was hurt real bad. Your mama was about your age at the time, but I don't think she ever really understood how bad her dad was injured. He had burns on his back and his legs. He never wore a pair of shorts or went without a shirt again."

"Was that the reason he got mean? Because he got hurt in the fire?"

"I suppose it was. After that day, Virgil was never the same. He was always taking something for the pain, but the real damage was in his head. He never forgave himself for failing that old woman. He blamed himself and he believed the other firemen blamed him, too."

"Did they?"

"I don't think so. It was just something that got stuck in his brain."

A noise sounded in the doorway. Winnie looked up to see Marly standing at the entrance to the porch. "A lot of people get hurt, Mother. It doesn't turn them into wife beaters."

"I don't suppose it does. But I couldn't leave him then . . . not when he was hurt."

"What about later? When he got worse? What about after he knocked you down and cracked your ribs? What about when he shoved you so hard you fell and broke your leg?"

Winnie squeezed her eyes closed, fighting not to remember. "There were things about your father . . . things no one knew but me. I knew how much he needed me. I—"

"*I* needed you, Mother. I was your daughter. I hated the way he treated you. I hated the fear we both felt whenever he came home drunk. I hated that there was nothing I could do to protect you."

But her brave daughter had tried. She had wound up with a black eye for her trouble and had to stay home from school. She had been too embarrassed to tell anyone what had happened.

Winnie had left him then, packed a couple of suitcases, and moved with Marly into a motel on the other side of the county.

But Virgil had found out where she was staying. He had come to the motel room, stood at the door and cried. He had begged her to forgive him, begged her to come back home. Winnie had never seen him cry, not ever, not even after the fire, when he had suffered such incredible pain. Virgil swore he would never lay a hand on Marly again, and he never broke his word.

Instead, he managed to take out his hostility on his wife, mostly when Marly wasn't home.

"I know the way you felt, dearest, but—"

Marly threw up her hands and walked back inside the house.

Katie didn't say a word, just focused her attention on peeling the apple in her hand.

Winnie sighed. Maybe she shouldn't have said anything. Clearly Marly hadn't told Katie much about Virgil, aside from what a terrible man he was.

But he hadn't always been that way, and those early years when they were together were what kept Winnie from leaving her husband when Marly had begged her to escape.

That, and her pity.

But those were secrets she had never revealed.

Winnie wasn't sure she ever would.

Emily scrubbed furiously at the crack between the countertop and the backsplash in the kitchen. Though she couldn't really see any dirt, she knew it was there, must have been there for years.

She pinched the scouring pad into a thinner shape and kept scrubbing. Her fingers were aching when the doorbell rang. Releasing a sigh at the unwanted intrusion, she tossed the pad on the counter and hurried for the door.

When she pulled it open, Patrick Murphy stood on the porch. "I thought I'd stop by. I didn't quite finish the flower beds when I was here yesterday."

"You've done more than enough, Pat. You don't have to feel obligated to come over here and weed just because you and Randy were friends."

"That isn't the reason. I mean, it's one of the reasons, but—" He broke off midsentence, his russet eyebrows drawing together as he noticed her hands. "You're bleeding. Your fingers . . . good God, Em, what happened?"

She shoved her hands behind her back, mortified he should see her broken nails and red, roughened skin.

Patrick reached out and caught her wrist, gently drew it toward him. She hadn't realized her cuticles were bleeding, the tips of her fingers rubbed raw.

"What were you doing, Emily?"

"I was cleaning. It's nothing." She tried to ease her hand away, but Patrick wouldn't let go.

"Come on," he said softly, "let's get this taken care of." Leading her into the kitchen, he spotted the steel-wool pad lying on the counter and the blue sudsy foam in the crack where she had been scrubbing.

Patrick didn't say a word. He just turned on the tap, took her hand, and eased it under the light stream of water.

"Well, you probably don't have to worry about infection," he finally said, examining the damaged area. "Not with all that soap." He took her other hand, which was also raw and bleeding, and stuck it under the tap.

"I told you I was cleaning," she said. "I guess I was rubbing a little too hard."

Patrick tore off a paper towel and carefully dried both her hands. His gaze went around the kitchen, and then he surveyed the living room. "Your house is spotless, Em. There isn't a speck of dirt anywhere."

"There's always dirt. It's a never-ending job."

"Only if you make it one." He tipped his head toward the bathroom. "You got any Band-Aids?"

"I don't need a Band-Aid. I'm fine."

He pinned her with a look.

"All right. They're in the bathroom. But try to be quiet, or you'll wake up Timmy. He's down for his afternoon nap."

Patrick made his way down the hall, walking quietly for a man of his size. He was only a little bigger than average, except for his hands and feet. She almost smiled. Every woman knew what they said about a man with big hands and feet.

Her smile slipped away. Dear God, she had only been a widow for six months! She was still in mourning. A good wife wouldn't be thinking those kinds of thoughts about another man, even if it was only an instant of humor.

Patrick returned with the box of bandages, stripped

the wrappers off a couple, and wrapped them around the ends of her injured fingers.

"They'll just get wet when I wash the dishes," she said.

Patrick looked her in the face. "I don't know what's going on with you, Em. I know something is. Have you given any thought to going back to work?"

She stared at him in horror.

"You used to love your job down at Suzy's. My cousin said you had a real knack for the business. Said the ladies came in especially to get your help in selecting an outfit."

Susan Norfolk, Patrick's cousin, was the owner of the shop. In Dreyerville, everyone knew someone who knew something about you.

"I'm a single mother now, Patrick. I can't go back to work."

"I realize you get an income from Randy's pension. That doesn't mean you can't have a job, too. Lots of women work and raise a family. There's no reason you can't be one of them."

She only shook her head.

Patrick sighed. "Promise me you'll think about it, okay?"

Oh, she would think about it. A dozen times a day

she thought about the job she had loved. But she had responsibilities. She had a job to do at home, as Randy had pointed out. She wasn't a wife anymore, but she was still a mother.

And no matter how hard it was, she was determined to be the best mother a woman could possibly be.

It was nearly the end of the day when Reed finally had a chance to pull the file on Virgil Maddox. Marly hadn't come right out and said so, but some sort of paternal abuse seemed a likely cause for the rift between mother and daughter.

The manila folder he pulled from the drawer held a mug shot of Virgil from an arrest nearly sixteen years ago. Marly would have been twelve years old. Virgil had been taken into custody for disturbing the peace, but the charges were dropped.

There was a family disturbance call a year later, phoned in by Nancy Cassidy, the neighbor who had lived in the house Reed now owned, but again, no formal arrest was made. Another couple of calls were resolved on-site.

Virgil's occupation was listed as firefighter with the Dreyerville Fire Department. Local deputies worked closely with the firefighters, and there was a lot of mutual respect. The officers would have gone out of their way to help Virgil, though Reed didn't think they would have ignored a clear case of spousal abuse if they had happened upon it.

Which meant Winnie had covered for her husband. She had somehow convinced the police that no abuse had taken place.

He didn't see any reference to Marly, which he hoped meant Virgil had never taken his bad temper out on his daughter. It still wasn't clear to him why Winnie and Marly had parted twelve years ago.

Maybe he would find out tonight.

He thought of the pretty little blonde who was visiting next door and found himself smiling. He was going out on a date. A real first date with a very attractive, very sexy young woman, the kind of date he hadn't had since he had met Carol.

Reed had fallen in love with his future wife the first time they had gone out, the night he had taken her to see *An Officer and a Gentleman* at the Arlington Theater downtown. At the end of the movie, when Richard Gere swung Debra Winger up in his arms and carried her off with him, Carol had cried. Reed knew then and there that she was the one. Attracted to her romantic nature and quiet intelligence, he had recognized the perfect fit they made.

And he had been right. Carol Constable was exactly the woman for him.

The thought made his smile slip away. He hadn't had a date since Carol had died. Not a real one. The kind where he anticipated the evening. The kind where he thought about the kiss he might get at the end of the night. Thought about what it might be like to take the lady to bed.

Thinking of Marly's slender, shapely figure set his blood pumping, reminding him that he was a man and that he had ignored the fact since he had lost Carol.

But he was coming back to life. Meeting Marly Hanson had somehow stirred the embers that had just began to flicker inside him, made him realize that life went on and that a man had no choice but to live it.

The smile returned as he glanced at the clock on the wall and the office manager walked up to his desk. "I gotta get going," he said to Millie. "I've got a date."

Her eyes widened. "A date? Really? Who is she?"

"You wouldn't know her. She's new in town. Well, actually, she moved away a while back, but she's home for a visit."

"That so?"

He didn't say more, though clearly, her curiosity was piqued. Everyone knew everyone in Dreyerville.

He wasn't ready for half the town to be discussing his business.

"Well, whoever she is," Millie said, "it's time you started getting out again."

And it was, he knew. After four years, it was way past time.

On the other hand, getting involved with a woman who would soon be leaving was probably not the best idea he ever had.

Of course, there was always a chance that Marly Hanson would decide to stay.

A notion that in some ways disturbed him even more.

~7~

Katie walked down the sidewalk next to Ham, Rufus sniffing the ground as he trailed along behind them. Ham had come over to the house after he got out of school. Grandma had dug out an old Scrabble game, and they had played out in the screened-in porch for a while. Ham was pretty good, but Katie had the advantage since she and her mother played word games all the time.

Besides, it was such a nice day, it seemed a waste to be inside.

"You want to see my tree house?" Ham had asked as the game came to a close.

"I'd love that."

He stood up from the table and reached for her hand. "Okay, come on."

Ham led her through the house, pausing long enough for Katie to tell her grandma where she was going, and they headed down the street. Ham told her that a couple of his friends had built the tree house up in an old sycamore in an empty lot at the end of the block.

"It's kind of our clubhouse, you know," Ham said. "Just me and Ben and Freddie. But sometimes we let in visitors."

"A clubhouse. I've never been in a clubhouse. It sounds really neat."

They reached the base of the big, sprawling tree that seemed to soar up into the sky. Though the branches were still bare, even when Katie craned her neck, the top was too high to see. Instead, she spotted the enclosed wooden platform the boys had built in the hollow where the branches fanned out. A sign on the side that read Private Property, No Trespassing, marked the spot.

"Can I go up?" she asked.

"Sure. But I have to go first and let down the ladder."

She stared back up at the tree. The trunk was bare, not even a branch for at least six feet. "How will you get up there?"

"It's kind of tricky. I'll show you." Taking a little jump, Ham stuck his fingers into a hole she hadn't noticed in the trunk above his head. He pulled himself up and then found a toehold nearby. The path up the tree was well worn, she realized, as Ham found a handhold here and foothold there, scrambling like a monkey up to the first branch, then on up from there. Opening the makeshift wooden door, he scrambled inside and came back out holding on to a long rope ladder.

"Stand back so I can throw it down."

Katie stepped out of the way, but as she did, she collided with a boy who had walked up behind her.

"Sorry," she said, her hand automatically raising to hold on to her pink knit cap.

"Look at this." The kid spun her around toward a second boy standing a few feet away. "Wonder what it is? A girl or a boy?"

The ladder came hurling down. "Leave her alone, Willie! You, too, Milo." Willie was pudgy and needed a haircut, his yellow T-shirt food-stained. Milo was skinny as a bone with a pushed-in face that made Rufus look handsome. Rufus barked as if he agreed.

Milo reached over and jerked off her pink knit cap. "It's a boy," he said, laughing.

"Nah," said Willie, "just an ugly girl. What happened to your hair? Your mama shave it off?"

Ham appeared just then and jerked Willie away from her. "I told you to leave her alone. You and Milo get out of here, or I swear you're going to regret it."

"Ham's got a girlfriend," the skinny boy chanted. "Ham's got a girlfriend."

"Yeah, only his girlfriend looks more like a boy," Willie said, laughing.

Katie looked at Ham and her chest squeezed. He was the first real friend she'd made since she had been sick, and now he would look at her the way the rest of the boys did. Her eyes filled with tears before she turned and started running back toward the house.

She might have kept going if she hadn't heard scuffling sounds behind her. A loud grunt and an *oof!* Then Rufus barked, and Katie stopped and turned just in time to see Ham punch Willie in the nose. Blood spurted out and Milo screamed as Ham spun him around and threatened to hit him, too.

"Get out of here!" Ham demanded, his hands still clenched into fists.

"You'll be sorry you did that," Willie sniveled, wiping away the blood streaming out of his nose. "My dad's the mayor. You can't hit me and get away with it!"

"Yeah!" Milo said. "Mayor Sanders will have you arrested."

Katie stood frozen as both boys turned and started running. Ham leaned down and picked up her knit cap, walked over, and handed it back to her. The tears in her eyes spilled onto her cheeks. Katie dashed them away with her fingers.

"You shouldn't have done that," she said. "You're going to be in so much trouble."

Ham blew out a breath. "Yeah, my dad's really gonna be mad."

She pulled the cap back on her head, covering her shiny skin. "None of my other friends would have stuck up for me like that."

Ham just shrugged. "They're idiots," he said.

Katie looked up at him and felt the tug of a small, slow smile. "Willie deserved it."

Ham looked down at her and grinned. "Yeah, he did."

Katie's smile widened. Turning away, she gazed wistfully up at the tree house. "I guess we better go home and tell your dad what happened."

Ham nodded, looking a little glum.

"Whatever he says, you're the best friend I've ever had."

Ham just smiled, but as they walked back down the sidewalk, she thought that his chest puffed out a little.

Reed picked up Marly exactly on time. She wasn't really surprised. The sheriff seemed an efficient sort of man. She wondered if he was really as steady and dependable as he seemed, the kind of man she had never really known.

Probably not.

In her experience, none of them were what they appeared to be. Except maybe Burly. The man was a womanizing loser when she had married him, and that never changed. She had never expected it would. But she had been desperate to escape her life in Dreyerville, and Burly had been her only hope.

"You ready?" Reed asked as he stood in the living room next to the door. Winnie stood a few feet away, a big smile on her face.

"As I'll ever be," Marly said mildly. But looking up at the handsome sheriff, she had to admit to feeling a little jolt of excitement.

As Reed opened the door, he turned back to Winnie. "We won't be too late."

"Don't be silly. Katie's fine here with me. Gives us a little more time to enjoy each other's company. You two stay out as late as you want."

Reed nodded. "Thanks, Winnie."

Marly felt his hand at her waist, guiding her through the door and across the porch. It was an old-fashioned gesture she found oddly charming. "I don't suppose we're going in the patrol car."

A corner of his mouth edged up. He had a very nice mouth. "I don't suppose."

Instead, he guided her toward a brown Chevy station wagon and held open the passenger-side door. Once she was settled, he rounded the car and slid behind the wheel. With his dark hair and suntanned skin, he looked good tonight in a pair of jeans and a yellow oxford-cloth, button-down shirt.

As she studied his profile, the solid jaw and nicely carved features, she felt a little flutter beneath her ribs. She tried to remember when that had last happened, but it had been too many years.

"So where are we going?" she asked.

He smiled, cast her a glance. "I made us a reservation at Barney's. You remember it, don't you?"

A slight pucker formed between her eyes as she tried to recall. "Is that the place out by the lake?"

"That's it. Good food. Not too fancy. I thought you might like looking out at the water."

"That sounds great." She leaned back in her seat. "Katie told me what happened today with Ham. Being the sheriff, I'm sure you weren't happy to have your son throwing punches."

"I gave him what for, I can tell you."

"I know it wasn't the best idea, but I appreciate the way he stood up for Katie."

Reed sighed. "The truth is, Willie Sanders is a bully.

From what Katie said, he deserved a good smack in the nose."

"What about the mayor? Will he be a problem for you?"

"I talked to him, told him the circumstances. I guess Willie had left out a few of the details. The mayor wasn't happy with his son's behavior. He said he'd talk to him again. I told him I'd already talked to Ham. In the end, we agreed it was best to let kids be kids."

Marly found herself smiling. "Ham's been wonderful to Katie."

"He's a good boy."

She noticed the confident way Reed handled the car and thought that this was probably his general approach to life. "I have a hunch you have a lot to do with Ham's behavior."

"I hope so. After his mother died, I tried to do my best, but it wasn't always easy."

"Believe me, I know. Being a single parent takes a lot of hard work."

Reed slowed to make the turn onto the highway leading out to the lake. "What about you? I don't suppose you've tried talking to your mom."

She straightened, feeling suddenly defensive. "Why would I? I tried to talk to her for years before I left home. She never wanted to hear what I had to say."

"Things are different now. Virgil is dead. Winnie hasn't suffered one of his beatings for years."

Her head jerked up. "She told you about that?"

He sliced her a glance. "No. I looked at Virgil's rap sheet. He was arrested sixteen years ago on a disturbing-the-peace charge. The charge was dropped, but officers were at the house on domestic disturbance calls a number of times over the years. No formal arrests were made, so I'm guessing Winnie covered for him."

Tension settled between her shoulders. She fought to hold back the painful memories. "That's right. No matter what he did, she wouldn't leave him. She ruined both our lives because of some warped sense of obligation to a man who beat the crap out of her whenever he felt the urge."

The car hit a bump in the road, but Reed's hold on the wheel didn't falter. "Is that the reason you ran off with Burly Hanson?"

None of this was any of his business, and yet she felt strangely compelled to answer, maybe even relieved to be asked. "There was nothing in the file about me and Burly Hanson."

"My office manager, Millie Caswell, is a longtime resident. After I read Virgil's rap sheet, I mentioned you to Millie. I guess her daughter knew Burly. Being raised here, you should know there aren't many secrets in Dreyerville."

Marly tucked a loose blond strand back into her neat French braid. "Not many, no. That's one of the reasons I'm glad I don't live here anymore."

"Privacy is always a problem in a town this small, but there are also a lot of advantages."

"Such as?"

"Good schools. Very little crime. You don't have to be afraid that if your daughter goes to the show with her friends one evening, someone is going to assault her."

It definitely wasn't Detroit, where she worried every time Katie was out of sight. "I suppose that's true."

"You don't miss it?"

She glanced over as Reed made the turn onto Lakeside Drive, the road that wound alongside the lake to the restaurant. "I miss it. Sometimes, when I'm in the city, I miss the quiet life, but I gave up most of my friends before I left. I didn't want anyone to know what was going on at home."

Reed said nothing more as he pulled into the parking lot in front of Barney's and turned off the engine. It occurred to her that she had already said far more than she had intended. She took a steadying breath as he rounded the front of the car and opened the door.

"No more questions, I promise." He helped her out of the car. "We're here to have a relaxing dinner. I didn't mean to make you uncomfortable. I guess asking questions is kind of a hazard of the job."

She released a slow breath, felt the tension drain from her shoulders. If she couldn't trust a sheriff to keep his word, the world was in a sorry state.

"I'm really getting hungry," he said, setting his hand once more at the small of her back. "How about you?"

Barney's loomed ahead of them, a dark brown wooden A-frame structure with a row of glass windows along the lake side of the building and a big wooden deck to sit out on during the summer.

Marly looked into those warm brown eyes and felt a faint lifting in her stomach. "Me, too." She smiled, beginning to look forward to the evening ahead. The past was behind her. In the fall, she would be starting a job as a full-time teacher, making a new life for herself.

They sat down at one of the wooden tables that looked out on the water, and a waitress came over and handed them a menu. Barney's was rustic; the walls were wood-paneled, and a large stone fireplace presided over one corner.

"The hamburgers are good," Reed said, looking over the menu. "So is the fried chicken."

"Fried chicken sounds great." The waitress returned with glasses of water, and they each gave her their order.

Marly sat back in her chair. "So what was she like?" She took a sip of water. "Your wife, I mean?"

"I guess you figure if I can ask questions, so can you."

She smiled. "That's exactly what I figure. Obviously, your marriage was nothing like mine. You loved your wife. What was she like?"

A fond smile touched his lips. "Carol was a romantic. I guess that's the word I'd pick to describe her. She always looked on the bright side of things. She made our life brighter because she was always optimistic."

"You were lucky."

"I know." He leaned back in his chair. "But she wasn't perfect. No one is. She spent too much money, and she never thought about the future. She just lived for the moment. We fought about it sometimes."

"Everybody fights, I suppose. Still, you were happy."

"I was. I think that to find real happiness, you have to look into yourself. I try to do that, more now that she's gone."

"Has it worked?"

"For the most part."

"My Katie is like that. That's how she survived those

terrible treatments. She's happy inside. And because she is, she makes me happy, too."

"Except when you're in Dreyerville."

She sighed. "It's hard being here. Too many memories." Marly glanced away, trying not to think of the past. Trying not to think of her mother and how much she had missed her.

Trying not to think how, deep in her heart where she rarely allowed herself to look, she wished things could be different.

~8~

"How was your date?"

Winnie stood at the counter, coffee pot in hand as her daughter walked into the kitchen the following morning.

Marly yawned behind her hand. "We had a very nice time."

Winnie filled a second mug with coffee. "You seem surprised." She carried it over to the table as Marly sat down still wearing her blue quilted robe.

"I suppose I am, a little. Generally, I don't feel comfortable with men."

She handed Marly the cup. "Because of your father."

Marly shrugged. "And Burly. I dated a math teacher for a while, but he was so full of himself, it drove me crazy. None of the guys I've dated were worth a damn." She took a drink of coffee. "The sheriff seems different."

"Maybe it's because he lost his wife."

"Maybe. We talked about her last night. Her name was Carol. I think he really loved her."

"They say a widower who's had a good marriage is happiest being married again."

"Maybe."

Winnie didn't press the issue. Her daughter was speaking more openly than at any time since she had come home. Maybe it was a good time for a little openness on her part, as well.

"Your father was that kind of man when I married him. The kind you could count on. I trusted him to be a good husband and to take care of us, and he did."

Marly quietly sipped her coffee. She didn't say anything, but at least she wasn't leaving the room.

Winnie sat down on the opposite side of the table. "Do you remember the way your dad was back then?" Her heart lifted at the memory. "Remember those picnics out at the lake? Lord, he used to love the outdoors. In the winter, we'd all go sledding."

Marly sipped her coffee.

"Remember the time he twisted his ankle trying to keep you from getting hurt when the sled turned over and both of you took a spill? His ankle swelled to the size of a melon. Do you remember any of that, honey?"

As she looked at Winnie, Marly's pretty blue eyes

filled. "Sometimes I remember. When I do, it makes the awful times seem even worse."

Winnie's heart squeezed. It took every ounce of her will to keep talking. "Even after the fire, there were good times. Like the day he took us horseback riding on his friend Jack Denton's old crow-bait nags."

Marly smiled. "I remember. It was a good day."

"I like to think of those times when I remember your father."

The smile slid from Marly's face. She stood up from the table. "I don't like to think of him at all. If we can't talk about something else, I'm going to leave."

"Please, don't do that, honey. I just . . . I want so much to fix things between us. As much as you hate it, it kind of seems like the only way it can happen is to tackle the past head-on."

Marly shook her head. "I can't, Mom. I wish I could, but I can't."

Winnie's chest tightened. For the first time, Marly had called her *Mom.* Winnie looked down at the mug of coffee in front of her, fighting to hold back the tears she didn't want her daughter to see.

"Katie's still sleeping," she said. "Why don't I fix you something to eat?"

Marly looked toward the bedroom. "It's the cancer

treatment, the radiation and chemo. Katie still gets tired pretty easily." She sat back down in her chair. "Thanks for the offer, but I'm not really hungry."

Winnie sipped her coffee. So far, Marly wasn't leaving and Winnie felt a growing ray of hope.

"How about a couple pieces of toast? I bought some of that white Wonder Bread you used to like. I'll pop a couple of slices in the toaster. It won't take a minute."

Marly grinned and shook her head. "I haven't eaten white bread in years. I try to stay healthy. Whole grains are a lot better for you."

Winnie grinned, too. "I hate white bread." She went over and opened a cupboard, took out a heavy, dark brown loaf.

"Mrs. Brenner down at the bakery started baking this and it's delicious. Has all kinds of seeds and nuts and things in it." She opened the plastic wrapper, took out two yeasty slices, and popped them into the toaster. "I've got some of my homemade raspberry jelly. You haven't stopped eating jelly, have you?"

Marly laughed. It was such a good sound to hear. "Are you kidding? You make the best raspberry jelly in the world."

Winnie's heart swelled. She managed to smile, but her throat felt tight. She busied herself making a stack of toast, pulled out the butter and jelly, and they sat together drinking coffee and eating the delicious bread.

Something was different this morning. Winnie couldn't exactly say what it was, but she couldn't help wondering if it had something to do with Marly's date last night with the handsome sheriff.

"So . . . are you going to see Sheriff Bennett again?"

Marly finished her last bite of toast. "He's taking me to the movies tonight. We're going to see *True Lies*. Arnold Schwarzenegger's in it and Jamie Lee Curtis. You okay babysitting Katie?"

"You know I am. That sweet little girl is the joy of my life. I can hardly imagine what it'll be like around here without her."

Marly's warm expression cooled. "I know what you're thinking, Mother. I enjoy Reed's company, but Katie and I are going back to Detroit. That's where I live, where I'm going to be working."

Winnie fought not to let her emotions show. "So, your job is right there in the city?"

"That's right. Chrysler Elementary. It's one of the best schools in the area. Teaching there is a great opportunity, and I need the money."

"Well, of course you have to work." But Winnie was already thinking of her friend in the Garden Club, Mabel

Simms, one of the teachers at Dreyerville Grammar School. Maybe they needed another teacher over there. Winnie was sure her daughter would be a very good one.

On the other hand, maybe the memories in Dreyerville were simply too painful. Maybe nothing she could do or say would keep her two beautiful girls from leaving.

If they did leave, Winnie wasn't convinced they would ever return.

And if they didn't, her heart would be broken all over again.

Marly was beginning to feel trapped, and she didn't like it.

She had been out with Reed almost every night since the barbecue at his house. Last Friday, they had all gone out together for pizza. Everyone but her mother, who had politely declined, saying she had promised to go over to her friend Opal's house to work on their program for the next meeting of the Dreyerville Garden Club.

Marly knew it was more than that. Winnie was hoping to see her daughter's relationship with Reed turn into something serious, maybe even permanent.

Worse yet, Marly found herself occasionally wishing the same thing.

She had managed to avoid him Saturday night, but

on Sunday, Winnie had insisted it was her turn for the barbecue, so Ham and Reed had come over for supper.

After that, Marly had weakened and gone out with him again on Tuesday. By the end of the evening, the attraction between them had grown even stronger.

"I need to kiss you, Marly," Reed had said as he walked her up onto the porch. "I can't wait any longer."

And then he turned her into his arms and claimed her mouth, and his lips were soft and yet somehow insistent, and a delicious warmth poured through her. Marly found herself kissing him back, her arms going around his neck. Reed had ended the kiss before she was ready, and she found herself smiling at that.

On Wednesday, they had parked at the lake and talked until late. And though she'd considered going farther than just harmless kissing, she wasn't ready for more and she didn't think Reed was, either.

She had never been seriously involved with a man. Burly certainly didn't count. She had slept with him because she owed him for marrying her. She was his wife, and a man had needs, something she had understood even when she had run off with him at sixteen.

But she had never enjoyed sex with Burly. Tolerated it, yes, but never looked forward to his nightly groping. Being a hopeful sort, she had tried again with the schoolteacher, but that was a bust. She had told herself she just wasn't a particularly passionate woman, but now that she'd spent time with Reed, she was beginning to wonder if maybe she was wrong. Just being in his company stirred wildly different emotions in her.

She was intrigued at the thought of making love with him. More than intrigued.

She was attracted to Reed Bennett. For the first time in her life, she understood what it was like to feel desire for a man. When he kissed her goodnight, she didn't want the kiss to end. When he held her hand, little tingles ran up her arm. When he laughed, she wanted to laugh with him. When he shared his thoughts and dreams, she found herself wanting to share her own, discovering in the process a few she hadn't realized she had.

Like helping Katie get through high school. Like sitting in the audience when her daughter graduated from college.

And deep down, she wanted more children. Watching Ham and Katie together had made her see that. And Reed had mentioned it. He'd said that he and Carol had tried to have more kids, but physically she wasn't able.

Marly was wildly attracted to him. Unfortunately, so was every woman in Dreyerville—or at least so it seemed. Wherever they went, women came up to the handsome sheriff on one pretext or another, and though he was always polite and seemed to take their interest in stride, she knew from experience how easy it was for a man to succumb to temptation.

She could very easily fall in love with Reed, and that would be a dangerous thing to do. She had seen what had happened to her mother, so blinded by love that she had let her husband destroy their family, let him grind his wife into the dirt at his feet. Marly thought of her own ill-fated marriage to Burly, who couldn't be faithful even if he had tried—which he never did.

She was never in love with Burly. If she fell in love with Reed, if she let down her guard and allowed herself to love him, count on him, depend on him to stand by her, she could be very badly hurt.

And the hurt would be passed on to her daughter.

She couldn't afford to let that happen. Unlike her mother, Marly would do anything to protect her child.

Feeling restless and moody, on Friday morning, she left Katie in the kitchen baking cookies with Winnie and drove out to the little mall at the edge of the city limits on the county road. It was almost ten, almost time for the mall to open.

There wasn't much to it, she recalled from her teenage years. A Sears department store, a Payless shoe store, a sporting goods store, and some women's dress shops. There was a Baskin-Robbins ice cream counter and an Orange Julius stand. She remembered a booth that sold giant pretzels slathered in cheddar cheese.

At least wandering around the mall would give her something to do besides sit in the library poring over a bunch of schoolbooks. If she didn't already know enough to teach fourth-grade kids, she was in trouble before she even started.

She parked the car in the lot, shoved through the mall doors, and walked inside. Memories assailed her. The last time she had been there, she had been a junior in high school. Her mother had taken her to the sporting goods store to look for a pair of athletic shoes to wear when she played tennis. But with her problems at home, she had quit the team early in the year and the shoes had never gotten much wear.

She spotted the store. Harvey's Sports, the sign read. She thought it was called something else twelve years ago, but she couldn't remember the name.

She ambled along inside the mall among the shoppers, just wandering, with no particular destination in mind. She didn't need anything, and she didn't really have any extra money to spend if she did. Still, it might be nice to buy Katie something.

There was no longer a Baskin-Robbins, she was disappointed to discover. Probably moved to a different location. Then the smell of hot pretzels reached her and she inhaled deeply, remembering the times she had come shopping with her mom and they had shared the treat. Apparently, the pretzel stand was still in business. She wandered in that direction, suddenly hungry.

"May I help you?" A skinny teenage girl with dark blond hair and crooked teeth spoke to her from behind the counter.

"Yes, thank you. I'd like a pretzel with cheddar, please."

The girl set to the task and, a few minutes later, handed Marly a pretzel with chunks of rock salt and rich orange cheese spread over it, nestled in a wax paper cone.

Marly thanked the girl, paid her, and took a bite, feeling the tangy rush of pleasure against her tongue.

"Marly?" The female voice was high and a little grating. "Marly Maddox, is that you?"

She didn't recognize the speaker, not right away, but when she turned, she saw Amy Singleton, one of the Dreyerville cheerleaders, still blond and petite and wearing expensive clothes.

"Amy Singleton. It's nice to see you."

"I'm Amy Richter now. Dan and I got married. You

remember Dan? He was the Panthers' varsity quarterback when we were juniors."

She remembered Dan. All the girls had had crushes on him, and he managed to get most of them into bed. Of course he would marry Amy, the prettiest girl in school.

"Actually, I saw you the other day at Barney's," Amy said. "But I wasn't sure it was you. You were with Sheriff Bennett."

"That's right."

Amy gave her the same catty smile Marly remembered from high school. "I was kind of surprised to see him there with you. He's been seeing Emily Carter, you know. She was married to one of his deputies, but Randy was killed. She's had a crush on Reed since high school, and now that her husband is dead, everyone's been speculating that Reed and Emily will get married—after a decent amount of time has passed, of course."

The delicious pretzel suddenly felt sour in her stomach. "Is that right?"

"Oh, yes. But that would probably be months away. In the meantime, it's only natural he would want to entertain himself."

Marly plastered a smile on her face. *Entertain himself.* Like Burly had *entertained himself* with the woman she had found in their bed.

"He lives next door to my mother," she said. "We're just friends."

"I see."

But Marly could tell by the knowing look on Amy's face that the gossip about her and Reed would soon be all over town. And everyone would believe that the wild girl who had run off with bad boy Burly Hanson was just fulfilling the sheriff's needs until a proper mourning period had passed and he could marry Emily Carter.

Marly clamped down on a shot of anger. Reed hadn't mentioned his involvement with the grieving widow. Typical male. He wasn't different from the others at all.

"Listen, Amy, I've got to run. It was really nice seeing you."

"You, too, Marly."

She turned away, the pretzel still in her hand. Her stomach churned. Thank God she had discovered the truth about Reed before it was too late.

She dropped the half-eaten pretzel into a nearby waste can and kept on walking. Her eyes burned. She refused to cry for Reed Bennett or any other man.

It was a lesson she had learned when she was sixteen.

Katie ruffled Rufus's wiry curls, and the dog barked and grinned. He was the funniest little guy. And so friendly. He seemed to know whenever she needed someone to talk to. Without even calling him, Rufus would jump the fence and come running up to her, his head cocked to the side, his dark eyes intent, his ears perked up as if he were ready to listen. Already Katie loved him.

She liked Ham, too. If she were older, she might think she had a crush on him. Her mother had said ten was still pretty young to be thinking about boys that way. But Ham was really cute, and he never made fun of her. She would never forget the way he had rescued her from those two gross boys.

And Grandma Winnie was great. That's what Katie called her. Grandma Winnie, not Grandma Maddox. That didn't sound right at all. Grandma Winnie was better than any grandma she had ever imagined. She never yelled, never got mad when stuff got spilled or when the cookies Katie was baking got burned on the bottom of the pan. She was the kind of grandma kids dreamed of having.

Katie was already dreading the day she and her mom would have to leave.

Rufus cocked his head in the opposite direction, and she realized she had said some of that stuff out loud.

"I don't want to go," she told the dog, who barked in agreement.

Grandma Winnie had told her she wanted them to stay at least two more weeks, wanted them to be here for Mother's Day. Katie didn't think her mom would agree. Mom always got sad on Mother's Day. Other mothers looked forward to their own particular day, but no matter what Katie did to make the day special, it never worked. Her mom would pretend to be pleased, but the sadness was always there in her eyes.

Katie sighed. It was Saturday. She wondered if her mom would go out tonight with Sheriff Bennett. Katie hoped so. She had never seen her mother as happy as she was when she was with him. She seemed more relaxed, not always on guard the way she was most of the time.

Wouldn't it be cool if the sheriff asked her mom to marry him?

It was a silly idea. They hardly even knew each other.

Katie smoothed Rufus's stiff curls. "I don't think she'd

say yes, even if he asked," she said. "She never does what she wants. She always finds some reason she can't." She looked wistfully back at the house. "Maybe I'll just tell her I don't want to go back, that I want us to stay here with Grandma and Ham and the sheriff. Maybe if I ask her really nice, she'll say yes."

But her mom had a job waiting in Detroit. She couldn't afford to give it up. They needed the money to pay the rent and buy food and stuff.

"I'm gonna miss you, boy." Katie ruffled the fur around Rufus's neck, adjusted his leather collar, and told herself Detroit wasn't that far away.

But once they left, Katie wasn't all that sure her mom would ever bring her back to Dreyerville again.

Reed left Ham battling it out with his friend Freddy Marvin in a furious game of Ping-Pong on the sunporch. Though he'd made Sloppy Joes for the boys, he hadn't eaten yet. He'd been looking forward to his date tonight with Marly, but she had called him at the office and canceled. He could tell by her tone that something was wrong and that it definitely had to do with him.

They had been together almost every night. The dates themselves had been nothing special, just out for a bite to eat or to take in a movie or to go for a walk beside the lake. Once, Marly suggested they go for a bike ride, which didn't turn out so well when her old, beat-up bicycle had gotten a flat on the way back home. It was fun just the same, and she had laughed and been a good sport about riding the ratty old bike she'd had since she was a kid.

In the beginning, it hadn't been easy to persuade her to keep going out with him, since she would be leaving soon and she didn't want to get "that involved." But eventually he had worn her down with his persistence, the way he did most everything.

His attraction to her had grown since that first evening on the way to Barney's, when she had started opening up to him. After seeing *True Lies,* they had talked some more. He had told her about how he'd felt after losing Carol and how much he had missed her, and Marly had revealed more about her life after she had run away with Burly Hanson. She seemed to trust him as she did few other men. At least that was what she'd said.

"If you can't trust a sheriff . . ." She had laughed and Reed loved the sound, rich and hearty and sincere. He loved the way her pretty blue eyes seemed to sparkle in a way they hadn't when he had first met her.

She had even been calling her mother *Mom.* Winnie had told him that. He didn't think Marly realized how much that meant to her mother. Or that in doing it, she had let down her guard a little, broken through some sort of personal barrier.

He thought of the phone call he had just now received and Marly's brusque tone of voice. Something was wrong. He could feel it. He'd always had good instincts, and they were screaming at him now.

The edginess he had been feeling grew worse. Knowing he should probably stay away, Reed crossed the living room and headed out of the house. The sun was sinking toward the horizon, reminding him of the date he no longer had. Striding across the lawn, he charged up Winnie's front-porch steps and reached up to bang on the door.

By sheer force of will, he made himself rap lightly. Marly peered through the window to see who was there, walked to the door, and pulled it open.

"What is it, Reed? I told you I wasn't feeling very well."

It had sounded like an excuse on the phone, and looking at Marly's tight features, he was even more certain of it now.

"I thought I'd better check on you . . . since you were feeling so poorly." Two could play the game, he thought, though it wasn't something he liked to do.

"I'll be fine. I just need a little rest."

"May I come in?"

"I'd rather you didn't. I might . . . might be contagious."

Under different circumstances, he would have smiled at her obvious attempt to get rid of him. Instead, he took a step forward, forcing her back inside the house. He'd been angry all day that she hadn't just told him what was wrong, and seeing her now, his temper sparked.

"All right, Marly, let's cut the bull. You're mad at me, and I want to know why. I thought we were having a great time together."

She rubbed her arms as if she were cold. "It doesn't matter. I'll be leaving the first of the week." There was something in her face, a sort of sad resolve.

"When people don't talk, it only makes things worse. You ought to know that better than anyone. Please, honey, tell me what's wrong."

Her head jerked up at the use of the endearment he hadn't meant to say. Her eyes glistened for an instant before her chin firmed.

"The truth is, we're getting too involved. I can't let that happen. I have to think of Katie. I have a substitute teaching job waiting in Detroit and a full-time position starting in the fall. Now, if you'll excuse me, there are things I need to do." She stood there waiting for him to leave.

His jaw hardened. He didn't want to go. He wanted to stay right there and have it out.

Unfortunately, his pager went off just then. *Millie.* He had to call the office.

"Looks like something's come up. I've got to go." He reached out and caught her shoulders, dragged her close and kissed her, quick and hard. "This isn't over, Marly. We're going to talk about this and figure it out. I'll be back."

She touched her bottom lip, still moist from his kiss, and opened her mouth to argue, but he was already striding away.

Something was wrong. He wasn't letting her leave Dreyerville until he knew what it was.

Reed's resolve hardened as he headed back to his house.

Winnie walked toward the back of the house, Katie skipping along beside her. They had been to King's Super to pick up some fresh vegetables and the makings for a blueberry pie. Marly had a date tonight with Reed, Winnie recalled. They would be gone by now. The thought made her smile.

While her daughter was out on a date with the handsome sheriff, Winnie planned to cook a meatloaf for Katie. Then the two of them would bake the pie.

Winnie climbed the back-porch steps, carrying the brown paper bag of groceries. She unlocked the back door, which Katie then held open.

"Thank you, sweetheart." She made her way into the kitchen and stopped at the sight of Marly sitting at the kitchen table.

"I thought you and Reed were going out."

"Something came up, and he had to cancel."

"Something at work?"

Marly glanced up. Her expression looked as dark as it had the day she'd first arrived. Things had changed since then, some of the darkness had faded, at least Winnie had thought so. Now she wasn't so sure.

"Me and Gran are gonna bake a pie," Katie said, pulling a small sack of flour out of the bag.

"Gran and I," Marly corrected.

"Gran and I." Katie left the bag on the counter and walked up in front of her. "Gran wants us to stay for Mother's Day. It's only another week. Can we, Mom?"

Marly started shaking her head even before Katie finished the sentence. "We're leaving on Monday, just like we planned. We need to get started on your tutoring so you can get caught up at school."

"We could start right here."

Marly came up out of her chair. "I'm sorry. I know you

want to stay, but it's time for us to go home." She walked out of the kitchen and into the living room and turned on the TV. Winnie followed.

"You seem upset, honey. Has something happened between you and Reed?"

"I don't want to talk about it, Mother."

Marly was back to calling her *Mother* instead of *Mom*. Winnie's chest hurt. She thought about pressing her daughter for more, but their relationship was so fragile she just didn't dare.

"I'd like you to stay, but I understand if you don't want to."

Marly made no reply.

Winnie's heart was aching, but she let the subject drop.

Her girls were leaving. She had known the time would come. She had just been hoping so hard . . .

Winnie turned away. The time with her girls was coming to an end. There was nothing she could do but accept it. Ignoring the lump in her throat, she pasted on a smile for Katie and walked back into the kitchen.

The next morning, Reed hammered on the front door of the gray frame house next door. He would have been back last night if it hadn't been for the hit-and-run accident down on West Adams across from the train station.

The victim, an elderly woman named Betsy Moses, was in the hospital. Fortunately, aside from a broken arm, it looked as if she was going to be okay.

One of his deputies, Patrick Murphy, had apprehended the driver of the old Ford pickup out on Highway 21. Frank Slattery had been drinking down at Al's Place. He was on his way home and didn't even know he had hit the woman. He was currently residing in the Dreyerville County Jail.

Reed took the steps up onto the porch two at a time. He had made himself wait until the respectable hour of ten A.M. before he'd come over, but it had taken every last shred of his patience.

His instincts were what made him a good sheriff. Something had happened to close Marly off from him. Reed was determined to know what it was.

He hammered again and the front door opened. He'd been expecting Winnie, but it was Marly who opened the door.

"We need to talk."

"There isn't anything to say."

He eased the door open wider and walked past her into the living room. "I'm not leaving until I know what's going on."

She took a deep breath, looking resigned. She was

dressed in jeans and sneakers and a pale blue cotton blouse. She looked beautiful. And tired. And he knew that somehow, he was the cause.

He glanced around the house, which seemed a little too quiet. "Where's Winnie and Katie?"

"Mother took Katie to the Farmer's Market."

"Good, then we can talk right here."

"I told you—"

"We're too old to play games, Marly. Just tell me what's going on."

Her chin firmed. She looked him dead in the face. "I found out about Emily."

Reed frowned, not quite following the conversation. "Emily? Emily Carter?"

"How many of them do you know?"

"I don't understand. What does Emily have to do with this?"

"Look, Reed, we've only known each other a little while. You don't owe me anything except honesty. That you do owe me."

"I'm lost here, Marly. I can't imagine what our going out has to do with Emily Carter."

"You aren't going to deny it, are you? Please don't do that, Reed. I've heard enough lies in my life. I can't take any more and especially not from you."

He raked a hand through his hair, trying to sort things out. "God, I wish I knew what you were thinking. Emily Carter is Randy Carter's widow. He was one of my deputies. About six months ago, he was killed in the line of duty. Are you thinking that something's going on between Emily and me? Because if you are, it just isn't true."

She crossed her arms over her breasts, which drew his eye in that direction and made him think of taking her to bed, which at the moment was *not* the right thing to be thinking.

"Come on, Reed. Everyone in town knows you're going to marry her."

He started shaking his head. Maybe he should have mentioned his visits to Emily, but it was just something he did for a friend and it never crossed his mind.

"Emily and I went to high school together. She has a little three-year-old boy named Timmy. I stop by to see them whenever I can, see if there's anything they need. The other guys do, too. I swear, that's all there is to it."

Her eyes found his, searching for the truth. "Amy Singleton says Emily's had a crush on you since high school. She says you're just waiting for a decent period of time before the two of you get married."

"I don't know how Emily felt about me in high school.

It isn't important. What matters is that Emily is just a friend. I understand the kind of loss she must be feeling, so I try to help her."

"That's it?"

"That's it."

"Then you aren't in love with her?"

"Hell, no." Since he rarely swore, her eyes widened. "Like I said, we're friends. Nothing more."

Marly bit her lip. She had the softest lips. He tried not to think of the kisses they had shared. Or the one he wanted to coax from her right now.

"I want to believe you," she said, a faint ray of hope creeping into her face. "I wish I didn't want it so badly."

He reached for her, gently cupped her cheek. "I'm not like the other men you've known, Marly. I'm not like your father or Burly. If I tell you something, you can count on it with your life. I'm telling you I'm not involved with Emily Carter. She's a wonderful young woman and a dedicated mother, but the only person I'm interested in is you."

Silence hung over the living room.

She swallowed, looked up at him. "I don't know how it happened," she said softly. "I didn't mean to let things go this far, but I care about you, Reed. I care way too much. I wish I didn't, but I do."

Relief and desire hit him in equal measures. Desire won out. Cradling her face in his hands, he bent his head and kissed her, just a tender melding of lips, a sweet sampling that only made him want more. When her mouth softened under his, the kiss deepened, grew more intimate, and he felt her tremble.

Marly might be tough on the outside, but inside she was sweet and vulnerable and passionate.

"I wouldn't hurt you and Katie for the world," he said softly, then simply gathered her into his arms. "We'll figure all of this out. We just need a little more time."

"We don't have time," she said against his cheek.

"We'll make time," he vowed.

He held her a moment more, finally let her go but kept hold of her hand. "Leave your mother a note. We're going for a drive. We'll talk things over. From now on, if either of us has a problem, we talk about it. That work for you?"

She just nodded, but there was the sweetest smile on her face. Something expanded in his chest. He was in big trouble here. Four years had passed since he had cared about a woman the way he did Marly Hanson. He hated to be thinking the L-word so soon, but he had a feeling that this was where he was headed.

He wanted her to stay in Dreyerville, to give them a chance to see where the attraction between them would lead. But there wasn't a chance of that happening unless she made peace with her mother.

Reed vowed he would help her find a way.

~ 10 ~

When she couldn't stand the house a minute more, Emily took Timmy shopping. They started downtown, stopping for a moment in front of the newspaper office to read the headlines of the *Morning News,* peering into the window of Tremont's Antiques, picking up from Culver's Dry Cleaning a favorite pair of slacks that had gotten a stain she couldn't remove. Careful to avoid Suzy's Boutique, she made a stop at Brenner's Bakery instead.

As usual, Mrs. Culver, silver-blond hair pulled back with combs on each side of her narrow face, stood behind the counter. Doris always had smile for her customers and an especially wide one for Timmy, who loved the bakery's glazed donuts.

"It's nice to see you, Emily," Mrs. Culver said. "When you worked at Suzy's, you came in all the time, but we don't see you much now that you're a homemaker."

"It keeps me pretty busy." That was a lie. She spent hours trying to figure out what to do with the long days she spent at home.

"You two having your usual? A glazed and a raisin bran muffin?"

She glanced down at Timmy, who was grinning and pointing through the glass at the donuts.

"Absolutely."

Mrs. Culver reached into the case and pulled out the baked goods. Emily reached into her purse and dug out her wallet to pay for the food.

"They sure do miss you over at the shop," Mrs. Culver said. "You haven't thought of going back to work, have you?"

"Not really." She let go of Timmy's hand long enough to hand him his donut, which he immediately stuffed into his mouth. "I've just got so much to do taking care of my son."

"I guess so. Still . . . Seems like, you know, with everything that's happened, it would be good for you to get out and about again."

"You've never had kids, Mrs. Culver. You don't realize how time-consuming they can be."

"I guess that's true." Mrs. Culver went to work wiping off the counter and Emily led Timmy over to one of the wrought-iron tables. She lifted the little boy into one of the chairs and sat down across from him.

Mrs. Culver didn't say any more, but as Emily ate the

muffin, she couldn't get the notion of returning to Suzy's out of her head. First Patrick Murphy. Now Doris Culver.

What if they were right? What if she could be a mother and still have a job? Randy didn't believe it. He had wanted her home every day. But when she was young, she had dreamed of being a fashion designer, and working in the boutique was in some small way a fulfillment of that dream.

Emily sighed. As soon as they finished eating, she wiped Timmy's hands and face with a napkin, tossed it into the trash can, and left the bakery. She was still not ready to face the empty house. Instead of going home, she drove to the mall just outside the city limits.

The parking lot was always busy on Saturdays, but she finally found a spot. Taking Timmy's hand, she led him through the automatic doors into the interior. She passed the Payless shoe store and Harvey's Sports. There were three ladies' dress shops, two on one side and one on the other, and she wandered in that direction.

Sarah's Trunk came first. It felt good to stroll among the dresses and scarves and ladies' handbags. The smell of leather mixed with the fragrance of perfume and the fresh scent of the starch in the garments. Pausing for a moment at the jewelry counter, she studied a rack that held earrings and necklaces in the new spring colors.

Yellow and pink were big this year, she saw, wishing she had a few new things in her closet. But all she really needed were a couple of spring scarves and a few new pieces of jewelry to update her wardrobe, and maybe a big summer purse.

She was looking at an oversize canvas bag in a bright shade of yellow, examining the zipper and the handy interior pockets that would be perfect for her lipstick and car keys, when the salesclerk walked up to the counter.

"May I help you?" She was twenty-two or -three, far younger than Emily's thirty-three years, tall and slender, with very short red hair and big hoop earrings, a look that was trendy and a nice change from the conservative styles most people wore in rural towns like Dreyerville.

"For the moment, I'm just looking," Emily said. Holding on to Timmy's hand, she tugged him over to a rack of dresses marked down 50 percent. One was a smart little paisley print that stood out among mostly heavier clothes left over from winter. Emily lifted it off the rack and held the hanger up in front of her, turned to survey herself in the mirror.

The sound of a woman's heels clicking on the floor drew her attention.

"Oh, what a darling little boy."

Emily looked up to see a woman in her early fifties,

well dressed in a simple blue gabardine pantsuit, attractive except for a faint scar that ran across her forehead near her hairline and trailed down to her temple. She smiled at Emily, then returned her attention to the child.

"Hi, sweetie, what's your name?"

"His name is Timmy," Emily said when her son just stared silently up at the older woman with his big brown eyes.

The woman knelt down to the little boy's height. "Hello, Timmy. My name is Anna."

Timmy turned away, clung to Emily's leg. "He's a little shy sometimes."

Anna rose. "I'm Anna McAllister."

"I'm Emily Carter. It's nice to meet you, Anna."

Anna studied the dress Emily had forgotten she still held in her hand.

"That's a really nice dress."

"It's half price."

"Well, you've found a real bargain there. Why don't you try it on?"

She wanted to. She hadn't had anything new since Randy died and she had quit her job at Suzy's. She didn't really have a place to wear it, but she loved clothes and at 50 percent off, the dress really *was* a bargain.

"I think I will." She tugged on Timmy's hand, trying to urge him toward the row of dressing rooms against the wall, but he was fascinated by the bright-colored jewelry on the counter and refused to budge.

"Come on, sweetheart." She tugged again, but his face crumpled. It looked as if any moment now, he was going to start crying.

When Anna handed him a string of yellow beads, he instantly brightened, smiling up at her with one of his endearing, crooked smiles.

"Go ahead," Anna said. "I'll watch him for a minute while you're gone. I raised two children of my own. I won't let him get into trouble."

Emily glanced toward the dressing room. It was only ten feet away. And it wouldn't take long. "Are you sure you don't mind?"

"Not at all."

"Thanks, I'll be right back." Slipping quietly off so Timmy wouldn't realize she was gone, she hurried over to one of the three dressing rooms and darted inside. It didn't take long to get her jeans and sweater off and pull the pretty little paisley dress on over her head.

It accented her curves and floated like a dream to just below her knees, which made her legs look really good. And at the markdown price, she could afford it. She told herself she didn't need it, that there was no one who would even notice the way she looked in it.

She twirled in front of the mirror. Maybe it was time she left behind the dark colors she had been wearing since Randy had died. For an instant, Patrick Murphy's face popped into her head, the wide smile he seemed to reserve especially for her, the concern she always saw in his eyes.

Horrified that she would think of him at all, she shook the image away, took off the dress, and hurriedly pulled on her beige slacks and pale blue, cotton knit sweater.

She couldn't have been gone more than five or six minutes when she returned to the jewelry counter. She was smiling, thinking that maybe in buying the dress, she was making the first step in regaining some kind of normal life. Then she realized Anna wasn't in the spot where she and Timmy had been standing.

Emily turned to survey the dress shop, certain the woman would be no more than a few feet away. Her gaze searched the narrow shop from one end to the other, but she saw no sign of Anna, or her son. Her heart was pounding, beginning to throb in that painful way it had when she had been married to Randy.

She rushed over to the salesclerk. "There . . . there was a woman . . . Anna McAllister. She was watching my son while I . . . while I tried on this dress." She held up the dress and realized her hand was shaking. "Did you see where . . . where they went?"

"The lady with the little boy?" the clerk said. "They were standing here a minute ago. When I looked up they were gone."

Emily was sure she was going to faint. "Please . . . you have to call 911. Call Sheriff Bennett. That . . . that woman . . . She stole my little boy."

The salesclerk's face went paper-white as she ran for the phone, and Emily raced for the door leading into the mall. Maybe they were waiting right outside. Maybe Anna was just a few feet away, looking into the window of another shop.

But no matter which direction Emily looked, there was no sign of Anna or her boy.

"Timmy!" She raced toward the far end of the mall. "Anna!"

She was out of breath and feeling light-headed when the security guard ran up to her. "What is it? What's happened?"

Emily's vision blurred with tears. "A lady named Anna McAllister . . . she . . . she's taken my son." And then the floor rushed up and the world went black and she didn't have to think that Randy had been right all along.

It was late Saturday afternoon. Reed sat across from Marly out at the lake, both of them cupping mugs of hot chocolate to warm their hands. It was colder today, still too chilly to sit out on the deck, but it was cozy inside the restaurant with a warm fire blazing in the big stone hearth.

Reed smiled at Marly, who smiled back at him over the rim of her cup, and his chest expanded. For hours, they had driven around just talking. It felt good to spend time with a woman after so many years. It felt particularly good to spend time with a woman he found so appealing.

He was grinning at her in a way he was sure made him look like a fool when his pager went off. Then his big, blocky cell phone sitting in the middle of the table started to ring.

Reed picked it up and held it against his ear. "Sheriff Bennett."

"Reed, it's Millie. There's been a kidnapping out at

the mall. Or at least that's the way it looks. It's Emily Carter's little boy." Reed's stomach went cold. "Emily says a woman named Anna McAllister took him. Deputy Wilcox responded to the call. And Deputy Murphy is on his way, as well. He insisted on going. I don't think a herd of wild horses could have stopped him."

"What have you got so far?"

"They found a car registered to Robert McAllister out in the parking lot. Robert is the woman's son. Since she didn't take the boy in the car, we think she's somewhere in the forest behind the mall. A female shopper on her way to her car confirmed it. She said she saw a woman and a child heading into the woods. She thought it was odd at the time. Patrick thinks we should ask for volunteers to help with the search."

"Good idea. Put the word out. Get the TV and news stations involved. Tell Murphy to start setting up a command post in the parking lot."

"Will do."

"I'm heading there now." He signed off and shoved back his chair.

"Something's come up. Might be a kidnapping."

"Oh, my God."

He turned to Barney Andersen, the owner of the restaurant, a big, blond Norwegian whose family had settled in the northern part of the state in the old logging days. "Hey, Barn, can you take Marly home? I've got an emergency."

"No problem, Sheriff." Barney tossed his rag up on the bar and started toward them.

"And put the word out, will you? Little Timmy Carter is missing. He was taken from his mother while they were in the mall. See if you can round up some volunteers to help with the search."

"You got it."

"Is that your friend Emily's son?" Marly asked as she rose from her chair.

Reed nodded grimly.

"I'll help, Reed." She looked over at Barney. "I'm going with Sheriff Bennett to help with the search."

Barney nodded. "I'll close up here, gather as many folks as I can, and be out there as quick as I can get there."

"Thanks, Barney."

The big Swede pulled his apron off over his head. "You just find that little boy."

Reed looked down at Marly and fought to control his emotions. "Let's go." He clenched his jaw. Emily had already suffered so much. He could only imagine how terrified she must be.

They crossed the parking lot. He unlocked the station wagon and opened the passenger door. As Marly climbed inside, he rounded the car to the driver's side. Reed slid behind the wheel, stuck his portable light on the roof of the car, and started the engine.

"I know how hard this must be for you, Reed." Marly looked over at him as they roared out of the parking lot. "But you have to believe this is going to turn out all right. It wouldn't be fair for Emily to lose both her husband and her little boy. God wouldn't do that to her."

Reed looked at her hard. "I'd appreciate it if you would remind Him of that, Marly. I'm sure Emily would appreciate your prayers."

Marly shook her head. "I'm afraid I stopped praying years ago."

He stepped on the gas and the car surged forward. "Then maybe now would be a good time to think about starting again."

Marly said nothing more as the car careened down the road. The landscape rushed past in a blur. He tried to fix his attention on the steps he would need to take once he reached his destination. But all the way to the mall, Reed prayed that little Timmy would be all right.

When he glanced toward the passenger seat, he saw

that Marly's head was bent and he realized she was praying, too.

That was the moment he fell completely in love with her.

Marly rode anxiously next to Reed. When they pulled into the mall parking lot, one of his deputies walked over to Reed's side of the car. The sheriff rolled down his window.

The deputy was an attractive man with a slightly crooked nose, hazel eyes, and brownish red hair. "We're getting the command post set up," he said, "and we've sealed off the area in case she went some other direction."

"Nothing turned up on your preliminary search?"

"We canvassed the mall. They weren't there. We found some footprints on the trail leading into the forest, but they disappeared in some rocks. We're ready to go back in as soon as we've got a search grid."

"What about the media?"

"Timmy's photo has been shown on the local TV stations, and the search has been announced on the radio, so we're getting a good turnout of volunteers. We're trying to get hold of a picture of the woman."

He tilted his head toward Marly. "Patrick Murphy, this is Marly Hanson, Winnie Maddox's daughter."

"Nice to meet you," Patrick said.

Marly leaned over and spoke through the window. "Same here."

Reed parked the car and they climbed out. A number of people had already arrived in the parking lot. Men and women milled in front of folding tables where maps were spread open and search grids were being laid out. More cars showed up by the minute. Half the town of Dreyerville, including several local college students, seemed to be there to volunteer for the search.

When someone needed help, it seemed everyone pitched in. But then, that was the kind of town it was. Marly had almost forgotten.

As the three of them crossed the lot, she spotted her mother's old white Buick easing into one of the spaces. Winnie and Katie climbed out and walked back to the trunk of the car. With help from one of the men, they carried a big blue plastic thermos over to one of the tables, hot coffee, Marly figured, for the volunteers.

Her mother seemed so different now, no longer afraid to be out among people. She had truly become part of the community, something Marly never would have expected. Winnie had always been too worried about what other people would think, what they would do if they discovered the truth about her abusive husband.

Winnie and Katie waved, and Marly waved back.

"Emily went in to try on a dress," Patrick told Reed as they walked along. "She was only gone a few minutes. The woman—Anna McAllister—volunteered to watch Timmy, but when Emily came out of the dressing room, both the woman and the boy were gone."

Deputy Murphy's worry was apparent. Marly remembered Reed telling her the deputies all watched out for Emily after her husband died. It was obvious she meant a good deal to Patrick Murphy.

Reed rested a hand on the deputy's shoulder. "We'll find them, Pat." Reed looked at Marly. "I need to talk to her."

"Of course."

Lines dug into his forehead as he headed for the woman sitting in a chair near one of the tables. She was petite and dark-haired, slender and pretty. Marly expected to feel a stab of jealousy, but it never came. Reed had said they were only friends, and she believed him. Instead, she felt a sharp pang of concern for Emily and her son.

Sitting in a lawn chair near one of the tables, the young woman looked pale and shaken, her eyes red-rimmed from crying. Someone had draped a brown wool blanket around her shoulders, but it didn't keep her from trembling.

Reed knelt next to her chair. "It's me, Em." He took

hold of her hand and she swiveled her head to look at him.

Her eyes filled with tears. "It's my fault, Reed. I left him with a woman I didn't know. What kind of mother would do that? What kind, Reed?"

"Patrick said she offered to watch him while you tried on a dress. You trusted her, that's all. It isn't always a bad thing to trust someone."

Emily's throat moved up and down. "Please . . . please find him, Reed. If something happens to Timmy . . . I don't . . . don't think I can go on."

Reed squeezed her hand and returned to his feet. "We'll find him, Em. We won't stop until we do."

She started crying and Reed motioned for Marly to come over. Before she had reached them, he headed for his men, determined to find the lost little boy.

"Hello, Emily," Marly said softly. "I'm . . . Marly Hanson. I'm a friend of Reed's."

She gazed up at Marly through her tears. "It's . . . it's nice to meet you. Reed told me about you when he . . . when he stopped by last week."

Marly managed to smile. Reed had told Emily about her. She had been right to trust him. "He thinks a lot of you, Emily. You and little Timmy. He won't let you down."

She nodded, but her lips trembled. "It's my fault this

happened. I shouldn't have left him alone with her. But Anna just seemed . . . she just seemed so nice." She started sobbing, and Marly knelt and caught hold of her hand.

"Maybe she is nice, Emily. Maybe something else is going on here, something we haven't figured out yet."

She swallowed. "It doesn't matter. It's still my fault. Randy said . . . said I was a bad mother. He . . . he was right."

Marly squeezed hard on Emily's hand, demanding her attention. "You said Reed told you about me. Did he also tell you about my daughter?" Emily's attention sharpened. "Did he tell you my Katie had cancer?" Marly turned, pointed to the little girl wearing the pink knit cap. "That's my Katie."

Emily's features softened. "She's beautiful."

"Yes, she is. But as hard as I tried to protect her, as much as I tried to be a good mother, I couldn't protect her from that terrible disease."

"Reed said . . . said she was going to get well."

"All of us are hoping that's true. The point is, Emily, things happen. Life happens. As mothers, we just try to do the best we can. Sometimes we make the wrong decisions, but it isn't because we're bad mothers. It's just the way life is."

Emily's pale blue eyes searched her face. "Do you really believe that?"

"Yes. Yes, I do. Give it some thought, will you?" Something moved at the edge of Marly's vision. When she glanced in that direction, she saw her mother standing next to Katie only a few feet away. Wordlessly, Winnie turned and led the little girl back to the coffee table.

Marly watched her go, certain her mother had overheard the conversation. Words that rang with a clarity like never before.

Mothers did the best they could. They didn't always make the right choices, but they did their very best.

Just as she had done with Katie. Just as Emily had done with little Timmy.

Just as her mother had done with her.

Marly's throat closed up and tears burned behind her eyes. So many years had passed. So many wasted years. Maybe it was time for that to change.

Led by the deputies and local police, Reed sent the volunteers into action. They would move in a line fifteen feet apart. If anyone saw anything, he or she was to call out. No one was to approach the woman. There was no way to know her mental state or what she might do to the child.

The line of volunteers began moving across the field toward the forest in the distance. Aside from the animal trails that meandered through the woods, it was dense and damp, white pines and cedar, maple and birch. Thick, green foliage blanketed the area, and a lush mat of ground cover made the landscape even more difficult to penetrate.

It was still chilly in April, but the sun was out, making it easier to see, and for that Reed was grateful.

Wishing he could search with the others, he remained at the command post, waiting for new information, hoping his men or one of the volunteers would come across the woman and the boy. Marly sat with Emily. Em had wanted to search with the others, but Reed had persuaded her to stay, saying that the McAllister woman might bring Timmy back to the mall and she would need to be there if that happened.

He thought that a little color had returned to Emily's pale cheeks and she had stopped trembling. Every few minutes, she would get up and walk around, then return to her chair and stare off toward the woods. He had tried to get her to go inside where it was warm, but she had refused.

A little ways away, Winnie and Katie and several members of the Garden Club were manning a table that held thermos bottles of hot coffee and stacks of paper cups, a place where people could warm themselves a little.

Ham and Freddy had ridden out with Freddy's dad. The boys were walking in the line between Patrick and Deputy Wilcox, close enough that the men could keep an eye on them. Rufus ran along beside the boys, sniffing the ground as if he searched as well.

When a call came in, Reed quickly picked up the phone.

"It's me," Millie said.

"What have you got?"

"We finally located Robert McAllister, Anna's son. He says his mother was in a car accident two years ago. She suffered some brain damage. He says she forgets things sometimes, sometimes gets confused. She's never done anything like this, but apparently, his brother lost a child about six months ago, a little boy about Timmy's age. He thinks Anna took Timmy because he reminded her of her grandson."

"We need to find both of them, and fast. I'm going to join the others. You won't be able to call me. There isn't any service out in the woods."

Reed signed off, gave the phone to one of the senior volunteers, and walked over to speak to Emily. He told her what they had found out about Anna McAllister.

"This is good news, Em," he said. "Anna isn't some kind of monster. I don't think she realizes what she's done."

Emily's head moved up and down as if she understood, but her eyes were glazed and he could read her fear. The forest was full of hazards, soft edges that could crumble away, hidden ponds, bears. The cold was biting, and that in itself was a hazard to a three-year-old child.

Marly reached over and squeezed Emily's hand. "Reed's going to find him," she said softly as he turned to leave.

Marly was right, Reed thought. He was going to find them. He just prayed it wouldn't be too late.

~ 12 ~

Marly wrapped her fingers around a paper cup half full of coffee, trying to warm her hands. She glanced over at Emily, who was now in the care of a group of deputies' wives. She should go inside the mall, get out of the chilly air, but like everyone else, she needed to be out here where she could watch for the return of the little lost boy.

"Marly? Oh, my God, it's you!"

She turned at the sound of the familiar voice, recognized her longtime friend, Peggy Ellis, one of her teammates on the high school tennis team.

"Peggy! It's wonderful to see you." They had written a few times over the years, but hadn't really stayed in touch. Four years ago, Peggy had been the one who had written to let her know her father had died of a heart attack.

Peggy leaned over and hugged her. "It's great to see you, too." They held on for a few extra moments. Peggy glanced over at Emily, who stood in a circle of women and yet seemed completely alone. "I wish the circumstances were different."

Marly's gaze went from Emily to the forest. "I guess everyone in town is out here looking for little Timmy." The volunteers were out of sight, marching through the dense vegetation.

"God, I hope they find him. Emily's had more than her share of grief this year."

"I know Reed will do everything in his power to bring Timmy back."

Peggy smiled. "Reed, is it? Not Sheriff Bennett?"

Marly shrugged. "We've been seeing each other. Unfortunately, I have a job back in Detroit, so I won't be staying in town much longer."

"That's too bad. The sheriff seems like a really great guy." She reached out and caught Marly's hand, gave it a quick squeeze. "I've really missed you over the years. You were the one person I could always talk to."

The simple words warmed her. "I felt that way about you, too. I didn't have many real friends back then. I treasured the friendship we shared."

"Well, you never know. Maybe you and the sheriff will fall madly in love and you'll move back home."

Marly felt a wistful pang. "Maybe." Coming back didn't sound as awful as it had when she had first arrived, and she was half in love with Reed already. But she wasn't the sort to jump into a relationship, not after what she had been through with Burly. Not after what her mother had suffered with Virgil.

And she had a life back in the city.

"Listen, I gotta run," Peggy said. She dug a piece of paper out of her purse and wrote her phone number down. "I'm single again, unfortunately. Still no kids, but I'm resilient. Call me if you get a chance."

Marly took the paper. It felt good to see Peggy after all these years. Strangely, they seemed to feel the same close connection they had when they were kids, as if only a few days had passed, not twelve long years. "I will," she said, "I promise."

Marly returned her attention to the tall trees and lush foliage of the forest. Reed was in there searching. She had come to admire and believe in him. Reed would find Emily's little boy.

For the second time in the last twelve years, she said a silent prayer.

Emily stared into the tall copse of trees that marked the entrance to the forest, her heart squeezing with fear and pain. The hours were slipping past. It would be getting dark soon. *Dear God,* she prayed, *don't let my little boy be lost out there in the dark all night.*

She wanted to be out there searching with the others,

but she knew Reed was right. She needed to stay where she was in case Anna brought Timmy back or some new information came to light.

The day was cold but the sun was bright. Someone had loaned her a pair of sunglasses as she stared out into the woods, searching with her eyes and heart instead of her feet.

Something moved at the edge of the clearing where the forest began. For a moment, she thought she had imagined it. Slowly, the image came into focus. One of the searchers was waving, another appeared, waving and shouting.

"We found him!" the man said. It was Floyd Culver, Doris Culver's husband.

Emily's heart clenched. Reverend Gains stepped out of the woods, waving his arms. She thought he was smiling, and her hope began to soar.

Joe Dixon and Bumper Murphy from over at Dixon's Garage appeared. "He's okay!" Joe called out, sliding an arm around his pretty new wife, Sylvia, who had also come to search.

Emily jumped up from her chair, straining to hear what the men were saying over the roaring in her ears and the pounding of her heart. Several more volunteers stumbled out of the woods. Emily started running. Her legs felt numb from sitting in the cold for so long, but she forced them to move toward the people streaming out from between the trees.

Then she saw him. Patrick Murphy held her little boy in his arms, propped against his chest. Timmy was wrapped in a blanket, and as she raced toward them, she saw that Patrick was grinning.

"He's all right, Em! Timmy's okay!"

She started crying then, racing toward the deputy, her heart threatening to pound its way through her ribs. "Timmy! Timmy!"

Patrick caught her against him when she stumbled, protecting her from the fall she might have taken.

"He's okay," Pat said.

She reached up to take hold of her boy, shaking so badly she was afraid she might drop him.

"Mommy!" He sniffed and she thought he would cry as she gathered him into her arms.

"I'm right here, honey."

"We couldn't find you, Mommy. Mrs. Anna got lost."

"I know. It's all right, baby. I've got you now."

Timmy clung to her. He was icy cold and shivering, but he wasn't crying. She smoothed the light brown hair standing up on his head and kissed his cold cheek.

"Let's get you both into the car where it's warm,"

Patrick said. "I'll drive you to the hospital so we can get Timmy checked out."

She looked up at him. "Do you really think that's necessary? He's been through so much already. I just . . . we just want to go home."

Patrick smoothed the little boy's hair. "He seemed fine when we found him. I think taking him in to his own doctor tomorrow would be all right."

She nodded, felt a sweep of relief. "Yes, that's a good idea."

"I'll get the car and turn on the heater. The two of you can climb inside and warm up."

He started to walk away, but she caught his arm. "Thank you, Patrick, for finding him. Thank you so much."

He reached out and touched her cheek. "I wouldn't have given up, Em. No matter how long it took."

Emily made no reply, but that soft touch somehow eased the tightness in her chest. She looked past him as he walked away, saw Reed coming out of the forest. Anna McAllister walked beside him. The legs of her gabardine pants suit were covered with mud, her brown hair no longer neat and tidy.

They walked straight over to where she stood still holding Timmy in her arms.

"I'm so sorry," Anna said. "I . . . I don't know what happened. One minute I was standing at the jewelry counter; the next, Timmy and I were in the woods. Only I thought he was my grandson, Nathan. Once I began to think clearly, I realized we were lost. You left your boy in my care, and I was frightened to death something would happen to him." Her eyes welled with tears and a broken sob escaped. "I'm so sorry. So terribly, terribly sorry."

Patrick drove the car up just then, saving Emily from a reply, which was good, since she had no idea what to say. Having once been a deputy's wife, she knew Reed would be taking Anna to the hospital for a mental evaluation. Even after what Anna had put her through, Emily felt sorry for the woman.

"You'd better get in where it's warm," Reed said. "Patrick can drive you and Timmy to the hospital."

"We're going home. We'll see the doctor tomorrow."

He nodded. "That's probably a good idea."

"What . . . what about my car?"

"We'll take care of it." Reed held up her car keys. "I dug them out of your purse." Which she had forgotten in her rush to reach Timmy.

Reed put the handbag on the seat beside her while she and Timmy settled themselves in the back of the sheriff's car. With the heater blasting, the hot air felt incredibly good.

She leaned down and kissed the top of her little boy's head. He was already asleep against her shoulder.

Patrick put the car in gear and started driving away. Through the rear window, she saw the people of Dreyerville waving, wishing them well. Tears burned her eyes, blurring her vision. Emily waved back, a silent thank-you for all of their help.

As the patrol car drove past where Reed stood next to Marly Hanson, Emily raised a hand in thanks for the words Marly had said.

A mother just does the best she can.

Emily looked down at the son she loved so much, and through her tears, she smiled.

~13~

Tired from a night of uneasy sleep, Marly walked into the kitchen Sunday morning. With the oven on, the kitchen felt warm and inviting. Her mother stood at the window, looking out at a day far more cheerful than the day before.

"Katie's out front talking to Megan Jeffries," her mother said, drawing her attention. "She lives three houses down. They met yesterday during the search and seemed to hit it off. Megan is really a sweet little girl."

Marly walked over to the window and looked out into the front yard. Katie was there, talking to a little girl with chin-length, silver-blond hair. Both of them were smiling, laughing as if they were already friends.

Marly's chest constricted. It was so good to see her daughter happy. After the illness, Katie hadn't seemed to know real joy until she got to Dreyerville.

"Are you ready for a cup of coffee, dearest?"

Marly thought of the decision she had made sometime during the night. "More than ready."

As Winnie walked over to pour them each a cup, Marly steeled herself for the conversation she was determined to have. It was past time she talked to her mother. There were things Marly needed to know. Things she needed to say.

It was time to set the past aside so both of them could move on with their lives.

Her mother filled two mugs and handed one of them over. Marly blew on the surface of the coffee to cool it but mostly to give herself some time. She took a sip of the rich, dark brew, felt the warmth of it sliding into her stomach. Not sure how to start, she just jumped in.

"It's been a long time since we really talked, Mom. I need to know . . . why did you stay with Daddy all those years?"

Caught off guard, Winnie raised her eyes to meet Marly's.

"I know you loved him," Marly persisted. "But now I realize you loved me, too."

Winnie's expression softened. "Of course I loved you, sweetheart. You were my child. My greatest joy. I would have given my life for you."

"You say that now, but what about then? Virgil was a drunk and an abuser. He hurt you time and again. I begged you to leave him. Every time the subject came up, we fought about it and you refused to go. You let him ruin both of our lives."

Winnie smiled softly. "But your life isn't ruined. Look at you. You've put yourself through college. You've become a teacher. You have a wonderful little girl. I knew that about you, Marly. I knew how strong you were. I believed you would make it, no matter what it took. But your father was weak. He needed me. Desperately."

"That's what you always said. *He needed you.* No matter what he did, you always came to his defense. You always protected him."

Her mother carried their cups over to the kitchen table and sat down. She looked as if she were trying to make a difficult decision.

"I swore I would never tell you this. I made a vow to your father. But Virgil's gone and it's time I made amends for the mistake I made not telling you all those years ago."

A little chill slid through her. Marly set her coffee mug on one of the round blue knit coasters her mother had sewn. "What was it, Mother? I really need to know."

"Virgil told me about his childhood. He said if I was going to marry him, it was only fair I knew the truth. You see, his mother—your grandmother—was . . . Rose Maddox sold herself for money."

Marly's eyes widened. "Rose was a prostitute?"

Winnie shook her head. "Not a streetwalker, nothing like that. Rose picked up men in bars, or in the café where she worked, places like that. She slept with them and in return, they gave her money."

Marly couldn't believe what she was hearing. She had never known her father's mother. Rose Maddox had died when Marly was still a baby.

"She didn't do it by choice," her mother continued. "She was in her thirties when she fell in love with a married man and got pregnant. There was no chance of him getting a divorce. She was a poor woman even then, and once she was carrying his child, he broke off with her completely. He never gave her a cent, and in those days, women couldn't just go down to the welfare office and pick up a check. Even a woman with a baby had to make it on her own."

Marly said nothing. She had never heard any of this before. She could hardly believe she was hearing it now.

"Rose was desperate. She had no way to buy food or pay rent. Virgil said there were days he went to school with nothing to eat but a biscuit made of flour and water. They lived in a tiny trailer out in the woods, and he slept on the floor. He was there even when his mother entertained her men . . . friends."

"Oh, my God." She had never known much about her

father, never known his secret past. "Go on . . . please." Her hands were shaking; she slid them beneath the table so her mother wouldn't see.

"I think Rose did the best she could, but times were hard. And as Virgil grew older, he reminded her too much of the man she had loved who had treated her so badly. Until Virgil and I met in high school, I don't think anyone had ever really loved him." Winnie smiled sadly. "But I did. I loved him from the day I met him. And I never cared about his past."

Marly's throat ached. "That's why you stayed. Because you loved him—and you pitied him."

"That's right. And because of the man he was before the fire. No matter what else he was, your father worked hard and always provided for us."

"Oh, Mom."

"Virgil had a heart condition. You didn't know that. He was a smoker, and of course, there was all that smoke from his job. The doctors warned him if he didn't quit he wouldn't last long. I told myself it would only be a couple more years until you went away to college. You wouldn't have to deal with him then. But I couldn't leave him. I couldn't hurt him the way his mother had."

Marly's eyes filled with tears.

"I made a mistake all those years ago. I should have

left him. Or maybe if I had explained, you would have understood."

Marly got up from her chair, and her mother rose as well. Marly walked toward her, opened her arms, and Winnie stepped into them. Both of them just held on. It felt so good, so right to be there. So many years had passed. All of them had suffered so much.

There were tears in their eyes when they finally let go.

"It's all so sad," Marly said, wiping the wetness from her cheeks.

"I don't think Virgil ever had a chance to be the man he should have been."

She thought of the father he had been before the fire and wondered if that might not be true.

Winnie reached out and took hold of her hand. "Will you and Katie stay for Mother's Day?" Her eyes were damp, her lips trembling. "Please say yes."

Marly's heart swelled. She didn't have to be back in Detroit until her summer school job started. "We'll stay. There's nowhere else on earth we'd rather be."

A sob came from her mother's throat. "I love you, dear child."

"I love you, too, Mom."

And because she did, she would never tell her mother what had happened that last night. The night Virgil had come drunkenly into her bedroom when she was pretending to sleep and fallen on top of her. As she struggled beneath him, she'd been terrified of what he meant to do.

"I love you, Winnie," he had said, and she realized he didn't know he was in the wrong room. "I need you. I need you so much."

Marly had shoved him off the bed so hard his head cracked against the wall. Then he lurched to his feet, staggered into the living room, and passed out on the sofa.

Winnie hadn't heard him come in, and since Marly didn't want to cause her mother any more heartache, she kept silent. She walked over to where her father lay and looked down at him. There was a time she had loved her dad so much. But she no longer knew this man he had become. She stifled a sob and told herself she had to be strong, had to do what needed to be done.

Aside from feeling shaken and out of hope, she was okay, but it was past time for her to leave. She knew for certain now that her mother would stay, no matter the pain she might suffer.

Marly had to escape. She couldn't save her mother, but she could save herself.

And maybe Virgil would treat her mother better if she wasn't there, always a thorn in his side.

That night, Marly had walked away.

It had taken twelve long years for her to return.

She looked at her mom, and the years fell away, the hurt and the pain, the sorrow and loss. Now only love shone between them.

A sweet ache rose inside her.

Marly was so very glad that she had come home.

Dreyerville

Mother's Day

Five Years Later

Winnie sat in a polished walnut pew in the lovely old Presbyterian church she had attended since she was a girl. Next to her, Marly sat beside her handsome sheriff husband. Their three-year-old boy, Matthew, perched beside Reed, and Katie sat next to Ham.

Marly had returned to church the Sunday after little Timmy had gotten lost and then been safely returned to his mother. They say the Lord works in strange ways, and Winnie believed it was true.

The events of that day had drawn Marly and Reed together, and they were so very happy. It seemed as if they were made for each other. Reed had once told Winnie he had known Marly was the right woman for him almost the moment he had met her. He loved her spirit and determination and her amazing resilience.

Winnie looked down the pew at her beautiful family. Katie's gleaming blond hair had grown back, and she wore it pulled into a neat little ponytail. Marly wore her soft curls loose around her shoulders, the way her husband liked it. Both Ham and Matthew had their father's good looks and thick, dark brown hair.

Katie's tests had all come back clear. She had made it five years cancer-free. Winnie's granddaughter was going to live a long, full life, another blessing to be thankful for on this Mother's Day Sunday.

Winnie glanced over at the pew to her right. Emily Murphy sat next to her husband, Patrick, and their son, Timmy, now eight years old. Three years ago, Emily and Patrick had married, and Patrick had formally adopted the little boy. Not long after the incident at the mall, Emily had gone back to work at Suzy's Boutique. She was the store manager now and did all of the buying. It was often remarked that Emily Murphy was responsible for making the ladies of Dreyerville the best-dressed women in the county.

Marly had said that Emily was worried about returning to work with a child to raise, but Patrick had encouraged her, and she did just fine holding down a job and taking care of her family.

Marly was also a working mother. Winnie's friend

Mabel Simms had recommended her for a teaching job at Dreyerville Grammar School. As Marly's relationship with Reed continued to blossom, she had decided to take the job. She was a very good teacher, and she loved working with the kids.

Winnie's gaze flicked to Reed. She saw him gently settle a hand on Marly's slightly rounded stomach. The pair looked at each other and grinned. Next year, with God's blessing, the Bennetts would have another child to bring to church on Sunday mornings.

Marly turned in Winnie's direction, reached over, and caught her hand. Neither of them took their relationship for granted. They loved each other, and they wouldn't let anything or anyone take that love away from them again.

"Happy Mother's Day," Marly whispered.

Winnie's eyes misted. "Happy Mother's Day, dear heart."

Lying on the front step outside the church door, Rufus's ears perked up as he listened to the sound of footsteps coming up the aisle. The service was over.

It was time for him to take his family home.

A SONG FOR MY MOTHER

As the years slip past and my mother grows old, I think how empty my life would have been if I hadn't returned to Dreyerville. If having a daughter of my own hadn't forced me to confront the past, to acknowledge the deep and abiding love I felt for my mother and to realize how deeply she loved me. How grateful I am that fate interceded and brought us back together, allowing me to tell her the way I felt.

How thankful I am that the song I wrote for my mother did not remain unsung.

AUTHOR'S NOTE

I'd like to thank you all for revisiting Dreyerville in *A Song for My Mother*, a story written about the special bond between mothers and their children.

Ionia, Michigan, was again my inspiration, a lovely little town in the heartland that in many ways seems not to have changed since the turn of the nineteenth century. If you enjoyed this book and haven't read *The Christmas Clock*, the first in my Dreyerville series, I hope you will look for it.

If inspiration strikes, it is my fond wish to write another Dreyerville story, perhaps one set around the Fourth of July, one of my favorite holidays.

Till then, all best wishes and happy reading.

Kat

A CONVERSATION WITH KAT MARTIN, AUTHOR OF *A SONG FOR MY MOTHER*

Q1. What was the inspiration for the title, *A Song for My Mother*? Is there a particular song that inspired you to write this novel about the complex relationships between mothers and their children?

  A: Actually, the title is a metaphor. It speaks to the trouble children have in communicating the love they feel for their parents. In this story, Marly has never expressed her love for her mother. As the tale begins, it is a song that remains unsung.

Q2. Readers of your previous book, *The Christmas Clock*, will be delighted to revisit the town of Dreyerville in this story. Did you know that you would return to this setting? Why? What does this town represent to you?

  A: I didn't start out with Dreyerville in mind for the second book, but after visiting the small Michigan town that is, in reality, Ionia, just east of Grand Rapids, I knew I wanted to go back. The charming, nineteenth-century village represents old-fashioned values, the days when honesty, courage, loyalty, and integrity were more valuable than they seem to be today. Eventually, I may do more Dreyerville stories.

Q3. What are some of the challenges of writing a novella versus a novel, and how did you deal with them?

A: As I tend to write sparsely in all of my books, writing a novella poses less of a problem for me, perhaps, than for other authors. I'm a person who loves brevity, which is clear in my novels. Less is more to me. In a story as poignant as this one, the novella works perhaps better than a full-length novel.

Q4. You have created wonderfully flawed female characters in *A Song for My Mother*. They have complicated relationships, make tough life-changing decisions, and are at times pretty hard on themselves. What do you hope to teach your readers through each of these extraordinary women?

A: I tend to think of women in general as being strong, tough, and solid—the sort often forced to deal with difficulty and make hard decisions. Maybe younger women haven't yet realized the problems they will likely face at some point in their lives. Perhaps a story like this teaches that whatever happens, they can face the situation and overcome it.

Q5. Marly and Emily are both mothers who also work outside the home. What are your thoughts about working mothers? Did you hope to portray them in a specific way in the book?

A: Having been raised by a working mother, I understand the difficulties faced by mothers who work outside the home. Being out in the real world, often being confronted with even greater challenges than their male counterparts, tends to make working women strong and resilient, just as Marly has become and Emily is becoming.

Q6. You tackle some tough subject matter such as alcohol abuse, death, and cancer while also sharing some very sweet and tender moments of love and family. What is your objective in showing such diverse life experiences?

A: As I answer these questions, the clearer it becomes that one of the underlying themes of the story is that life makes us stronger. And I am fairly certain that almost all of us share very diverse and often difficult life experiences. Perhaps reading about other people's experiences makes our own problems more bearable.

Q7. There are three grieving widows or widowers in the book: Reed, Winnie, and Emily. But each character copes with his or her own loss in a different way. What is the message in the book about dealing with painful memories and facing life's challenges?

A: I hope the message is that whatever helps us get through the tough times is all right. It doesn't matter how we deal with grief as long as it helps us get through it. That is what life is about. Living, dying, and just carrying on in the face of adversity.

Q8. Do you think *A Song for My Mother* would make a good Mother's Day gift? Why?

A: I think it would be a very nice gift. The book says what children and parents often can't find a way to say to each other. It talks about enduring love, the kind that bridges the difficult gaps that sometimes develop between family members over the years. Aside from that, it's an uplifting, feel-good story. Which, with so many problems in the world today, is always the best kind, I think.

Q9. Winnie makes a decision early in the book to protect her daughter from her father's secret past. Do you think all mothers should do whatever they can to protect their children from adversity, or is it better to confront hardships as they come our way?

A: It is probably better to confront hardships when they happen, but as Winnie believed about Marly, sometimes a child isn't ready to deal with difficult truths until she is older and perhaps a little wiser.

Q10. If you could sum up the message in *A Song for My Mother,* what would it be?

A: Being a parent is a difficult task. There are no maps, no guidelines. Parents have to find their own way, do the best they can. The decisions they make are not always the right ones, but that doesn't mean they don't love their children. And it is that bond between parent and child that holds a family together.

Enjoy reading samples
from two novels by *New York Times*
bestselling author Kat Martin

Against the Law

A NOVEL

He had everything he ever wanted. Plenty of money. A successful security business. A sprawling, custom-built home in the Sonoran Desert north of Scottsdale filled with pricey original works of art.

Devlin Raines had it all. Yet lately he'd begun to feel dissatisfied.

Soaking up the rays of the early-October sunshine, the perfect time of year in Arizona, Dev adjusted his wrap-around sunglasses and stretched out on the chaise lounge beside the swimming pool. He had almost drifted off when his friend and employee, Townsend Emory, shoved open the sliding glass door.

"Sorry to bother you, boss. There's a woman here to see you. She's damned insistent." Town was a big, black former tackle for the Arizona Cardinals. Fourteen years ago, a neck injury had ended his career. Fortunately, the man had brains as well as brawn and now worked at the house, handling Dev's personal affairs.

Dev pushed his sunglasses up on his head and frowned at his friend, who took up a good portion of the doorway. He had a standing rule. None of the women he dated came to the house without calling first, which saved a lot of embarrassment if another woman happened to be there. In his no-strings relationships, the rule had worked fairly well.

So far.

Swinging his long legs to the ground beside the chaise, he stood up, wondering who it was and why she so urgently wanted to see him.

"Hey, wait a minute!" he heard Town say as a tall, shapely brunette sailed past him out onto the patio. "You can't just barge in here!"

The woman ignored him and just kept walking. "You must be Devlin Raines." She flashed him a bright, self-assured smile and extended a slender hand with nicely manicured, hot-pink nails. She was around five-nine, with very dark, jaw-length, red-streaked, upturned, fly-away hair. She was wearing skinny jeans and a pair of strappy, open-toed, red spike heels.

He'd never seen this woman before. She wasn't wearing a wedding ring. And she was sexy as hell.

"I'm Raines." He flicked a glance at Town, telling him the situation was under control, and the big man slipped silently back inside the house. "What can I do for you, Ms.? . . ."

"Delaney. Lark Delaney. I came here to hire you, Mr. Raines. I'm hoping you'll be able to help me."

She was more than just sexy. She was a bombshell. Just not in the usual sense. This woman oozed energy and purpose. She was flashy yet somehow stylish with her big silver hoop earrings and oversized, pewter-trimmed, paisley purse.

She wasn't the sort he preferred. He usually went for a pretty little bit of arm candy who did whatever he told her. Yet he felt the pull of attraction as he hadn't in a very long time.

He reached out and lifted his short-sleeved Tommy Bahama shirt off the back of a patio chair and shrugged it on, covering his bare chest and a portion of the navy blue Speedo he was wearing, probably a good idea considering his train of thought.

"Why don't we sit down over there in the shade?" He pointed to a huge covered patio that looked more like a living room, with a fully complete, top-of-the-line outdoor kitchen. The day was pleasantly warm but not so hot that the automatic misters attached to the perimeter had come on.

They sat down in yellow overstuffed chairs around a big table inlaid with colorful mosaic tiles.

"So, Lark . . . how did you know where to find me?"

It wasn't common knowledge, though he had certainly had enough parties here for word to get out. And of course, there were the ladies he brought home on occasion.

"Actually, I stopped by your office in Phoenix. When they said you weren't in all that often, I came out here. A friend of yours recommended you. Clive Monroe. He gave me your address. He said the two of you served together in the army. He said you were Rangers."

Clive "Madman" Monroe was more than a friend. He had once saved Dev's life. "You're here to hire a private investigator?"

"That's right."

"Didn't Clive tell you I'm retired?" After leaving the army, Dev had invested the money he'd saved in the stock market. He'd been one of the winners, then gotten even luckier when he'd invested in Wildcat Oil. He and his brothers, Jackson and Gabe, had won big on that one.

Lark smiled. She had very full lips and they were painted the same hot-pink shade as her nails. His mind flashed on the erotic things lips like that could do to a man, but he forced the thought away.

"Clive said you'd help me. He said you owed him a favor."

More than a favor. If it hadn't been for the precisely placed round from Monroe's M4 carbine, Dev wouldn't be lounging around the pool right now.

"So . . . are you and Clive . . . involved?" he found himself asking.

Her eyes widened. Big green cat-eyes that made the rest of her pretty face even more striking. "No. Actually, Clive recently married. His wife and I are friends—Molly Harris, before she became Molly Monroe."

"I hadn't heard."

"It was kind of a whirlwind romance. Molly's how I met Clive. He's a great guy. And he seems to think very highly of you."

"That's nice to hear. But like I said, I'm retired." *Mostly.* Though at the moment, coming out of retirement to spend a little time with Lark Delaney sounded like a very good idea.

"Clive said you'd help me."

Dev blew out a breath. There was no real choice in the matter. He owed Madman Monroe. Clive had never asked for any kind of payback. The favor of working with a gorgeous brunette—even if she was 180 degrees from his usual type—didn't seem like too much to ask.

"So what can I do for you, Ms. Delaney?"

She leaned forward in her chair. She wasn't overly

endowed in the bosom department, but she had more than enough to suit him.

"I liked it better when you called me Lark, and it's kind of a long story. I'm not exactly sure where to begin."

"Let's start with what it is you'd like me to investigate."

"I need to find my sister's baby. A little girl. She was adopted four years ago. The files were all closed, the proceedings kept secret. But it was my sister's dying wish that I find her daughter and make sure she's being raised in a good, loving home."

"Your sister is deceased?"

She nodded. For an instant, her pretty green eyes clouded. "Heather was only twenty-one, five years younger than I am. She lived here in Phoenix. She died of breast cancer three months ago. I spent the last few weeks with her. As I said, finding her daughter was her dying wish."

"So you want to hire me to locate the family who adopted the child."

"I want to hire you to help *me* find them. I need to do this myself. I need to be involved. I promised Heather. I won't let her down again."

"Have you tried the Internet?" Dev asked. "There are dozens of sites that specialize in locating birth parents, adoptees, that kind of thing."

"I've tried the Web, believe me. Geneology.about .com. OmniTrace. GovtRegistry.com. Miraclesearch. I just don't have enough information."

Interesting lady, Dev thought. A brain, as well as a luscious little body. Too bad it looked as if he was going to be working for her. Getting involved with a client was one rule he never broke. He owed Monroe. But working with a woman as sexy as Lark would definitely be a test of his willpower.

He looked her over, and a corner of his mouth inched up. His debt to Madman was about to be paid in full.

The
Christmas Clock

A NOVEL

Prologue

There are years in our lives that change us, mold us forever in some way. I was eight years old that Christmas, too young to really understand all the undercurrents swirling around me.

It is only now, fourteen years later, as I graduate from Michigan State University and prepare for a job in the health care industry, that I am able to look back with the clarity to see that Christmas for the miracle it truly was.

Back then, during that summer of 1994, with the trees leafed out and the sun warming my shoulders through a T-shirt that hung down to my knees, I didn't realize disaster lay just a few months ahead. I only knew I wanted to buy the beautiful clock in the window of Tremont's Antiques as a gift for my grandmother, Lottie Sparks.

I didn't know that in trying to buy the clock, I would meet the people who would change my world, and my life would never be the same.

CHAPTER 1

August 1994

Sylvia Winters was going home. She had been back to the small Michigan town of Dreyerville only once in the past eight years. Her mother's funeral had demanded a return, but she had left the following day. Only a few close friends had attended the brief, graveside service held at the Greenhaven Cemetery. Marsha Winters had started drinking the day her husband disappeared. Abandoned with a month-old baby in a ramshackle house at the edge of town, she took up the bottle and didn't put it down for twenty years. Neither she nor Syl ever saw Syl's father again.

Times had been hard back then, but the years Syl had spent in the charming rural community surrounded by forested, rolling hills held memories she cherished. She was a good student, and she was popular. In high school, a glowing future spread out before her: a scholarship to college and a career in nursing, a husband and children, the sort of life Syl had always dreamed of and never had.

But life was never predictable, she had learned, and oftentimes cruel. At nineteen, during her first year at Dreyerville Community College, Syl had fallen in love. She and Joe Dixon, the school's star quarterback, were engaged to be married the summer of the following year. Syl couldn't imagine ever being happier.

Then her world came crashing down around her, and all of her dreams along with it. A routine doctor's appointment had brought news so grim that the week before the ceremony, Syl called off the wedding. She packed her belongings that same afternoon and left for Chicago.

If it hadn't been for her mother's sister, Bessie, Syl wasn't sure she would have made it. Aunt Bess and Syl's dearest friend, Mary McGinnis Webster, had been responsible for getting her through the most difficult time of her life.

But things were different now.

Syl studied the double yellow line in the middle of the two-lane highway leading into Dreyerville. The air conditioner hummed inside the car, while outside, the temperature was hot and a little humid this late in the summer. Dense growths of leafy green trees lined both sides of the road, and a narrow stream wove its way through the grasses, bubbling and frothing in places, lazy and meandering in others.

As she drove her newly washed white Honda Civic toward the turn onto Main Street, a feeling of homecoming expanded in her chest. She recognized Barnett's Feed and Seed, just down the road from Murdock's Auto Repair at the edge of town.

Making a left onto Main, she spotted the old domed courthouse built in 1910 and the ornate clock tower in the middle of the grassy town square. A little farther down the street, Culver's Dry Cleaning held the middle spot in the long, two-story brick building that filled the block on the left, and there was Tremont's Antiques, right next to Brenner's Bakery.

Sylvia smiled. The apartment she had just rented sat above the garage at Doris Culver's house. Doris worked at Brenner's Bakery, had for years. The middle-aged woman was practically a fixture behind the counter of the shop.

Syl's friend Mary had found her the apartment. A job as a nurse in a local doctor's office had recently appeared in the employment section of the Dreyerville *Morning News*, and Mary had convinced her to send in an application. After flying out for an interview, Sylvia had gotten the job.

She was coming home at last. She wasn't sure what sort of life she could make for herself in the town she once had fled, but something told her coming back was the only way she could conquer the demons that had haunted her for the past eight years.

* * *

Doris Culver didn't believe in happily ever after. She hadn't since she was nineteen, madly in love, and found her boyfriend, Ronnie Munns, in the backseat of his parents' '55 Chevy with Martha Gladstone, the local librarian. Love, Doris believed after that, was for fools and dreamers, and she never allowed herself to succumb to its lure again.

At fifty-six, Doris Culver felt old, but then she had for most of her life. Her husband, Floyd, the retired owner of Culver's Dry Cleaning, was a nondescript, balding man who wore horn-rimmed glasses and built birdhouses to fill up his empty days. Floyd was six years older than Doris, whom he had met when she came into his store with an armload of laundry. After cleaning her clothes for nearly five years, Floyd asked Doris out on a date. This July 5th, they had celebrated twenty-two years of marriage.

Doris felt as if it were fifty.

She rarely saw her husband except at dinner, which he ate mostly in silence. Afterward, he returned to his woodshop in the garage at the back of the house, where he stayed until he trudged up to bed at exactly nine P.M.

Though the sale of Floyd's business three years ago had provided them with a comfortable living, Doris had kept her job at the bakery, where she had been employed for years. She loved her job, especially decorating the cakes and cookies the shop made for holidays and other special occasions. With little else to fill her time, she went to work early and usually stayed past closing. Afterward, she returned to her two-bedroom, white stucco house on Maple Street, cooked Floyd's dinner, cleared the dishes, and spent the rest of the evening painting ceramics.

It was a consuming hobby. Every table, every bookshelf, even the window sills, held miniature clowns, birds, horses, dogs, cats, vases, and pitchers all done in the bright colors Doris used in an effort to cheer up her lonely world. Instead, somehow the crowded rows of objects, often in need of dusting, only made the house more oppressive.

Doris was glad for the hours she spent at the bakery, where the fragrant aroma of chocolate-chip cookies and fresh-baked bread was enough to buoy her spirits.

The shop on Main next to Tremont's Antiques was a narrow brick building with big picture windows painted with the name Brenner's Bakery in wide, sculpted gold letters. Frank Brenner had died sixteen years ago, but the bakery, now owned by his son, remained a landmark in Dreyerville.

It was Saturday morning. Doris stood behind the counter wiping crumbs off the top when the bell chimed above the door, indicating the arrival of a customer. She tucked a strand of gray hair dyed blond under her pink-and-white cap and smiled at her next-door neighbor and her grandson, Lottie and Teddy Sparks, as they walked into the shop.

"Good morning," Doris beamed. "How are you and Teddy today?"

Lottie set her shopping bag down on a little iron chair. "Darned arthritis has been acting up some, but aside from that, both of us are fine." She looked down with affection at her grandson. "We're kind of hungry, though." Lottie was wrinkled and slightly stoop-shouldered and her hair was as white as paper. Still, there was always a sparkle in her eyes and the hint of rose in her cheeks.

Doris smiled. "Well, we can certainly take care of that." She turned toward the dark-haired, fair-skinned boy, who looked up at her with big brown, soulful eyes. "So what's it going to be, Teddy? A glazed or a maple bar?" It was a Saturday morning tradition. Doris always looked forward to seeing Lottie, who had once been her fifth-grade teacher.

The pair lived in the yellow-and-white wood-framed house on Maple Street next door to Doris, but they didn't get to visit much, not with the hours Doris worked. But she had always admired Lottie Sparks, and Teddy was purely a treasure.

The child stared into the case that was filled with donuts: jelly, chocolate frosted with walnuts, powdered, and crumb. There were also bear claws and all manner of coffee cake rings. He nibbled his lower lip, then pointed toward the top shelf of the case.

"A maple bar, please."

"My, that does sound good." Doris plucked a piece of waxed paper from the box on the counter, reached into the case, and drew out a fat, maple-frosted bar. "Here you go, Teddy."

The little boy grinned. "Thank you, Mrs. Culver."

Lottie ordered a cinnamon roll, and Doris handed it over on another sheet of waxed paper. When Lottie turned to leave, Doris reminded her that she had forgotten to pay for her purchase.

"Silly of me." Lottie reached into her handbag for the little plastic coin purse she always carried. She asked again how much she owed, then dug through the money to find the right change, fumbling with this coin and that until she finally put the money up on the counter and Doris picked out the sum she needed.

Doris watched the woman cross the room, feeling a hint of concern. Lottie was getting more and more forgetful. Doris couldn't help wondering what would happen to Teddy if the old woman's memory continued to get worse.

The pair sat down at one of the small, round tables in front of the window to savor their purchases, and Doris watched with only a small twinge of jealousy as the boy looked up and smiled so sweetly at his grandmother.

When Doris had married Floyd at thirty-four, she was already too old to have a child, or at least she had thought so at the time. Floyd, whose two boys by a previous marriage were living with their mother in Florida, didn't really care. Occasionally, Doris wondered if, all those years ago, she had made the right decision, but deep down she knew that she was never cut out to raise a child.

Grandmother and grandson finished their treats and got up from the little round table. Doris waved good-bye as they tossed their used waxed paper and napkins into the trash can and walked out the door. She thought of Teddy and the mother he had lost four years ago, the reason he now lived with Lottie. If he lost his grandmother as well . . .

She shook her head, worried what the boy's future might hold.

* * *

Lottie exchanged places with her grandson on the sidewalk, positioning herself between him and the light passage of Dreyerville traffic on Main Street. At seventy-one, Lottie never would have suspected she would be raising an eight-year-old boy, though it shouldn't have surprised her.

Her only daughter, Wilma, had never been the responsible sort. In her early teens, Wilma had run away from home more than once. She missed school, and started smoking in secret when she was fourteen. Lottie found her drunk the first time two years later. The girl had graduated high school by the sheer force of Lottie's will, though she never went on to college as Lottie had hoped.

Instead, at the age of thirty-seven, after two failed marriages and a string of deadbeat, live-in boyfriends, Wilma had wound up pregnant by the married man she was dating. Four years later, after drinking and partying with a friend, she had lost control of her car on her way home and died when she hit a tree.

Lottie had wound up with Teddy, but he wasn't a burden. The boy had become the joy of her life.

As they walked along the sidewalk, she felt his small hand in hers and smiled. Glancing ahead, her steps began to slow and Teddy came to a halt beside her. Both of them looked into the window of Tremont's Antiques, a favorite place to visit on their Saturday morning outings. Today, they didn't go in, but Lottie could see the small Victorian hand-painted clock she had been admiring for nearly a year.

"It's still there, Gramma."

"Yes, I see it is." Lottie loved clocks. She owned four beautiful antique clocks she had purchased over the years and a big grandfather clock her late husband, Chester, had bought for her on their fortieth wedding anniversary.

But this little clock was special. It reminded her of the one her mother had on the wall in the kitchen when she was a little girl. She used to sit at the old oak table and watch the hands move over the face while her mother baked cookies. The clock at Tremont's reminded her of the happy days of her childhood, memories that were rapidly fading.

Lottie's chest tightened with sudden despair. Something terrible was happening to her, something she couldn't fight and simply could not stop.

Two years ago, she had been diagnosed with Alzheimer's disease. At first the signs were subtle: misplacing objects, forgetting the date right after she had looked at the calendar, not remembering little words like *cat* or *comb*, saying another word in its place. Worried, she had gone to see her longtime family physician, Dr. Waller. He had referred her to a doctor named Davis, who specialized in Alzheimer's cases.

Several visits that included a medical history of her family, a physical examination, a brain scan, and a mental status evaluation revealed the truth. She had a very progressive form of Alzheimer's, a type of dementia that destroyed brain cells and robbed the mind of memory. She could expect the symptoms to worsen at a very rapid pace, and she needed to be prepared. Eventually, the disease would kill her.

Lottie looked down at Teddy, who was staring up at her with big, worried brown eyes.

"Gramma? Are you all right?"

How long had she been standing there? She had no idea. She managed a smile for Teddy. "I'm fine, sweetheart. Why don't we go on home?"

Teddy looked relieved. Lottie gazed off down the street, which suddenly seemed less familiar. Their house was located two blocks farther down Main, then left on Maple Street. So far, she hadn't forgotten how to get there, but the doctors had warned her it could happen.

Teddy took her hand as they started walking. She let him lead the way. She wondered if he had noticed the subtle changes coming over her, and she suspected that he had. Lottie was a deeply religious woman. She was ready to meet her maker, though she would have preferred another path to glory. She would go without complaint, but there was Teddy to consider.

Her husband had passed away eight years ago. Her sister and daughter were dead. She had some distant cousins, but they were more feeble than she and certainly not suitable parents for an eight-year-old boy. For the past two years, ever since she had learned of her condition, Lottie had been hoping to find an answer to the problem of Teddy's future.

Before it was too late, she had to find Teddy a home.

CHAPTER 2

Syl was supposed to meet Mrs. Culver at one o'clock on Saturday to get a key to her new apartment. Arriving a little early, she drove around for a while, enjoying the feeling of homecoming, grateful that few changes had been made in the little town she since had moved away.

At a few minutes before one, she pulled up in front of the house on Maple Street. Driving a Volvo station wagon, Doris Culver pulled in right behind her. Syl watched her climb out of her car, thinking the woman looked exactly the way Syl remembered but thinner and paler, her gray-blond hair a little wispier.

"Welcome back," Mrs. Culver said, handing her the key. "I hope you like the place all right."

Syl smiled. "It'll be all mine. That's a first for me—which means I'm sure to like it."

Mrs. Culver insisted she call her Doris and also

insisted on helping carry Syl's belongings up to her newly acquired quarters above the garage.

"You can do whatever you want with it," Doris said as they climbed the stairs. "Make it feel like it's your own."

"Thank you."

"You don't have any pets, do you?"

She had never had a pet. Why did it suddenly seem as if she had missed something? "I'm afraid not."

One of Doris's blond eyebrows went up. "Well, small animals are okay, if you decide to get one."

Syl smiled, liking the notion. "Maybe I will."

Doris started back down the stairs to her house, a gray wood-framed home built in the thirties, then stopped and turned.

"Tomorrow's Sunday. I go to the Presbyterian church over on Elm. Maybe you'd like to come with me."

Syl hadn't been to church since she had left Dreyerville. Why not, she thought. She was making a new beginning. Maybe starting back to church was a good idea.

"Thank you, I'd like that very much."

"Service starts at eleven."

Syl just nodded. Already her life was changing. Or perhaps it was only changing back.

A shiver ran through her. When she had left Dreyerville, she'd been engaged to Joe Dixon. Four years ago,

Mary had written to tell her that Joe had moved back to town. Syl knew he had spent the previous three years in prison. She also knew that she was the cause.

Her stomach tightened. Sooner or later, she was bound to run into him. She had no idea what he might say to her or what she might say to him, but maybe facing Joe was part of the reason she had come back.

At least their meeting wouldn't be today and, with luck, probably not tomorrow, since Joe wasn't much of a churchgoer, or at least he hadn't been, back then.

With her car unloaded, she closed the apartment door behind her and turned to survey her domain: living room, kitchen with eating area, two bedrooms, and a bath, more than enough room for her. The place was furnished, which was good, because she had been living with her aunt and didn't own much except for her clothes and a few treasured personal possessions.

When she had first arrived in Chicago, she had stayed with Aunt Bess because she needed her aunt's help and support. Two years ago, the tables had turned and it was Bess who needed her. She had suffered a debilitating stroke; then six months ago, the woman who'd been far more a mother than Syl's own had died at the age of fifty-two.

That was when Syl began thinking of home, imagining

what it might be like to return. Then Mary had phoned, and now she was here.

* * *

Doris usually went to church by herself. Each week, she asked Floyd to go with her, but there was always something more important he had to do.

They used to go together each week, but over the years, Floyd accompanied her less and less. Today, she left him working, boring a hole in the front of one of the little wooden birdhouses he built out in his shop behind the house. Floyd sold them down at Barnett's Feed and Seed, the local mercantile, and a couple of other places in town, more to feel useful in his retirement than for the extra income he earned.

Dressed in her favorite pink linen suit, Doris waited at the bottom of the stairs leading up to the apartment she had rented to Sylvia Winters, and a few minutes later, the girl came hurrying down the steps. She was smaller than Doris, about five feet four, and pretty, with short honey-brown hair that curled softly around her face, and light green eyes.

"I hope I'm not late."

"I'm a little early. Are you ready?"

"I sure am."

They got into Doris's station wagon and drove over to the Presbyterian church. It was humid, the sun heating the air and dampness seeping into Doris's clothes. A small crowd gathered near the door, forming a circle around the minister, the Reverend Thomas Gains, who stood on the steps of the white wooden building with its tall white steeple. Lottie parked the car, and she and Sylvia walked over to join the group.

"Good morning, Doris," Reverend Gains welcomed her. "I see you've brought a friend."

"I'm Sylvia Winters. I just moved back to town." Sylvia held out a slim hand, and the reverend shook it.

"It's nice to meet you. I hope we'll see you often."

He turned back to Doris. "How is Floyd?" The minister always asked this question, and it always embarrassed her.

"He's fine. Had a bit of a headache this morning. I'll give him your regards."

"Please do."

She thought of Floyd at work in his dusty shop and cast a glance at Sylvia. They made their way inside the church.

* * *

Mondays were always busy. Joe Dixon wiped his hands on an old grease rag and tossed it up on the shelf. All three bays at Murdock's Auto Repair were full of cars, and there were several more waiting outside. Murdock's was the best garage for miles around, and people lined up for service.

Joe smiled at the thought. Being a mechanic was a dirty, greasy, noisy job, and he loved every minute of it. Since he'd been a sophomore in high school, he had dabbled with cars. In his senior year, he had run across an old '66 Chevy Super Sport headed for the junkyard, bought it for a song, and overhauled it with his dad's help, turning it into the big red muscle car it was back in its day.

He'd worked two jobs that summer to pay for the parts he needed, most of which came from the junkyard meant to be the car's final resting spot.

That success had pointed him toward a career in auto mechanics. He had known even then he wanted to own his own shop, and now, at twenty-nine, he was finally on the way to making it happen. In the four years since his return to Dreyerville, he had become half owner of Murdock's garage. He would own the whole business by the time Bumper Murdock was ready to retire.

The phone rang and Joe walked over and picked up the receiver. It was Mrs. Murphy, one of his customers.

"Joe, I can't get my car started," she said. "I think the battery is dead. I'm supposed to be at choir practice in half an hour. What should I do?"

"I've got to finish checking the oil for a guy in the waiting room, then I'll come on over. I'll give you a ride to church and then take care of your car."

A sigh of relief whispered over the phone. "Thanks, Joe."

He smiled. "See you in a couple of minutes."

Hurrying toward the sporty little yellow convertible that belonged to Jim Higgins, one of the male nurses at the hospital, he checked the oil, and added a quart.

"How much do I owe you?" Jim asked.

"Just the price of the oil."

"Great. Thanks, Joe."

"Glad to help."

Thinking of Mrs. Murphy as he strode toward his truck, he glanced around the shop. If things had been different, he would already have owned the business. He wouldn't have wasted three years of his life in the state penitentiary.

Or in fairness, maybe he would have wound up there, anyway. He'd been a hothead back then, as good with his fists as he was with his hands when he worked on a car.

Still, it was Syl's disappearance that had set events in motion.

A muscle clenched in his jaw. Sylvia Winters, the woman he had loved, had nearly destroyed his life.

* * *

It was Monday. Lottie knew because the repair shop called to remind her of her appointment. After making sure Teddy fastened his seatbelt, Lottie backed the car into the alley behind the house. It was a 1984 Mercury Topaz that Chester had purchased two years before he died. She didn't drive it much, only to the doctor's office or to King's Supermarket or, as today, to the repair shop.

Chester had always taken the car to Murdock's Auto Repair on Main at the edge of town, so she went there, too. A nice young man named Joe Dixon did most of the work there now, and he seemed to be honest, never over-charging, always finishing the work on schedule.

Lottie couldn't remember for sure if she had called Joe on Friday or another day in the week, but this morning she had found the note she had placed beneath the red plastic magnet on her refrigerator, reminding her of her ten o'clock appointment to have the oil changed. It was summer vacation, so Teddy was home from school and Lottie was enjoying his company.

Still, the confused state she often found herself in was occurring more and more often, and she didn't like the idea of Teddy seeing her that way. Concentrating on the road, Lottie saw the repair shop on the right-hand side, signaled, and pulled into a parking space in front of the building.

* * *

Joe Dixon spotted the faded blue metallic Mercury at the same time Bumper Murdock called out the news.

"Mrs. Sparks is here." Bumper checked off the appointment on his clipboard. "Which bay do you want her in?"

Joe waved to the little white-haired woman barely visible behind the wheel of her car. He had been taking care of Lottie Sparks's auto for years. The Merc was in tip-top condition. It was its owner who had started to fade.

"The middle bay is good," Joe said, waiting while Bumper gave directions for Lottie to line up the car and drive it onto the lift. Her grandson was with her, Joe saw, remembering that school was out for the summer. The little boy must be seven or eight, dark hair, dark eyes, cute little guy, smart as a whip. Joe had always loved children, boys or girls, it didn't really matter.

Being a stone's throw from thirty, he had imagined

himself married by now and raising a passel of kids. Instead, he was single, a loner who rarely dated or even went out. Joe frowned as memories of Syl and him began to pour in. He shoved them back into a corner and went over to speak to Lottie Sparks.

He was working on the Mercury twenty minutes later, Lottie in the waiting room sipping a cup of coffee, when little Teddy wandered into the service area. The kid's neck swiveled around as he took in the grease guns, tool boards, tire changers, and air guns. His brown eyes fixed on Bumper, who was working on a Toyota, the left rear wheel jacked into the air while Bumper used the air gun to remove the nuts from the wheel.

The kid stood unmoving, transfixed by the loud buzzing sounds and how easily the wheel came off. Bumper rolled the tire over to the changer, and Teddy's gaze moved off in another direction.

"What kinda car is that?" He pointed toward Joe's prize possession, a black-and-white '64 Thunderbird convertible, a big four-seater with long, sleek fins. Joe only drove it once in a while, but he had really enjoyed fixing it up.

"That's a T-bird, son. They don't make 'em like that anymore."

"Can I see inside?"

Joe flicked a glance at Lottie, who seemed content where she sat on the brown vinyl sofa in the waiting room, and tilted his head toward the car. "Sure, why not?"

Teddy grinned and raced over. One of his eye teeth was missing, though his front two had come in, a sign that the boy was growing up.

"You get a quarter from the tooth fairy for that?" Joe asked.

Teddy looked up at him. "She came for these two." He pointed at his two front teeth. "I got fifty cents. Gramma said the fairy would come for this one, but she didn't. I guess she forgot."

More likely the tooth fairy being Lottie Sparks had forgotten. Joe had noticed that the old woman was becoming more and more forgetful.

He opened the driver's-side door of the T-bird and motioned for Teddy to climb in behind the wheel.

"Wow, this is great." The kid was too small to see out, but he sat there grinning, leaning back in the red leather seat.

"Yeah, pretty great." Joe reached down and ruffled the little boy's hair. "You like cars, Teddy?"

"I love 'em. I'm gonna have a really fast car when I grow up."

Joe laughed. He could remember thinking that same

thing. His second car had been a hot '82 Camaro with a custom grill and a four-speed manual transmission. Little Teddy would have loved it.

Joe smiled at the memory and helped the boy climb down from the car. "We're just about done with the Merc. Tell your grandmother it'll only be a few more minutes."

Teddy didn't move. "I was thinking . . . I been raking up leaves for Mrs. Culver—the lady in the house next door to ours. And I'm weeding for Mr. Stillwater across the street. Do you think you might have some work I could do?"

Joe shook his head. "Sorry, kid. A garage isn't a good place for someone your age. Too much heavy equipment. Too many ways you might get hurt."

The boy's face fell. He gazed around the shop like it was Disneyland and he couldn't get a ticket to get in. "I need to make some money so I can buy my gramma a present."

"Yeah? What kind of present?"

"A clock. She loves it. She always stops to look at it when we go to town. I'm saving up so I can buy it for her for Christmas."

Joe thought of the woman in the other room. From what Bumper had told him, Lottie Sparks was all the family the little boy had. Mother dead. No father. No man at all in the family.

Teddy was studying the engine Joe was working on in the corner. Joe knew it was stupid, but all of a sudden there he was, opening his mouth, probably letting himself in for trouble.

"I'll tell you what. You go ask your grandmother. If it's all right with her, you can work a couple of hours a day cleaning up around here."

Teddy grinned, flashing the hole where his tooth should have been. He turned and raced off toward the waiting room and a few minutes later, Lottie Sparks walked in.

"Teddy says you want to hire him."

"I know this isn't the best place for a kid to work, Mrs. Sparks, but I promise not to let him come in here where we keep the heavy equipment, not unless I'm with him."

"It isn't good for a boy to be around an old woman all the time. He could use a man's guidance. You just make sure he doesn't get hurt."

"I'll keep a real close eye on him, Mrs. Sparks."

"He can ride his bike down here. It's only a few blocks. Long as he goes the back way, there won't be any traffic."

"That sounds good. If he wants, he can start tomorrow afternoon."

Teddy was grinning again. "What time, Mr. Dixon?"

"How about ten till noon? And it's Joe, not Mr. Dixon. And that guy over there, that's Bumper."

"Bumper?" Teddy turned toward the stout man walking toward them. Bumper was almost twice Joe's age, looking forward to an early retirement. At five feet nine, he was five inches shorter than Joe and built like a fireplug. "That's a funny name," Teddy said.

"They started calling him that when he was a kid," Joe explained. He and Bumper's son, Charlie, were best friends, had been since they were freshmen at Dreyerville High.

"Because he liked cars?" Teddy asked.

Because, according to Charlie, he was pudgy as a kid and always running into things. But Joe just said, "Yeah, Bumper's a top mechanic."

Teddy looked up at Bumper with awe but made no comment. The man beneath the grease-stained overalls was still a little chunky, but not like the old days, at least according to Charlie.

The Merc was finished. Joe backed the car out of the garage and waited while Mrs. Sparks and Teddy climbed in.

As he watched them drive away, he thought of all the problems a kid Teddy's age could cause, how much time watching the boy would take, and marveled at the crazy things he sometimes got himself into.